All Around the Mulberry Bush

By

ROBERT H. ROWLAND

To Silas & Ronaldle for nearly a lifetime of love and friendship,

Bob

LIGHTHOUSE PUBLISHING COMPANY
CORONA, CALIFORNIA

"Life will not be easy, nor will it be all love and kisses. We'll have hard and tough times. But I believe, deep in my heart, that our love is strong enough to get us through those times. Together, with God's help, we will make it." Taken from a love letter from Sherman Rowland to Betty Houston. It was written October 19, 1920 shortly after they became engaged. Betty was teaching school in Smithville, Oklahoma, and Sherman was farming at Erick, Oklahoma. They did have hard and tough times. But, their love got them through all those times for over fifty-five years.

This book is the story by their fourth child, Robert, during two of those hard and tough years. It is a story of the Great Depression years when hope gave way to hopelessness and when dreams were smashed by drought and sand storms. It tells of honest souls seeking answers to life's greatest questions in a variety of religious experiences in a Sunday school in a country schoolhouse and in churches of a small town. In spite of hardships and disappointments, faith and laughter carried the families through.

Robert Rowland's family migrated from Oklahoma to California during the Great Depression. They lived in migrant farm worker's camps from Holtville to Madera for four years. He graduated from Madera High School and holds degrees from Pepperdine University and Harding University. He became a high school baseball and basketball coach, principal and a college dean. At 32 he became the youngest college president in the nation. He later served as president of the American Citizenship Center at Oklahoma Christian University. While there he was awarded six Principal National Awards from Freedom's Foundation. Five were for the nation's best campus-based citizenship education programs and one was for public address. In 1972, he was selected as one of the Outstanding Educators of America. He is a lecturer, the author of four books and numerous articles on religion, government, citizenship and the U.S. Constitution.

Mr. Rowland married Joye Cooper of McAlester, Oklahoma, in 1947. They have a son, Robert, and a daughter, Cynthia Rowland McClure. In addition they have four grandchildren, Uriah and Dannielle Rowland, and Micah and Caleb McClure.

This book is dedicated to the heroic struggles of Mid-American families during the Great Depression. Those who struggled and lost, being forced to leave families, friends and farms to move westward in the hopes of survival in California. It is also dedicated to those who stayed behind and struggled against almost overwhelming odds as the dust storms swept across Kansas, Oklahoma, Arkansas and Texas. They stayed on making heroic survival efforts fighting grasshoppers, drought and poverty.

In spite of their struggles each group kept a sense of humor and maintained their faith in God and country. Many would not have survived had their county not provided some of life's essentials under the New Deal created by President Franklin D. Roosevelt. Many would not have wanted to survive without a deep faith in the living and loving God who gave them hope.

Table of Contents

— CHAPTER ONE —
THE MULBERRY BUSH

The mulberry bush was located between our big and little chicken houses. The big chicken house was halfway to the barn and the little chicken house was halfway to the windmill and the water tanks. The big chicken house never held chickens. It was used for the storage of feed grains, next year's seed and hand tools. The little chicken house was where the chickens roosted at night and had nests where the hens laid their eggs during the day.

The mulberry bush was really more of a tree than a bush. It served three purposes. On summer days it was big enough to give some shade. In the spring it yielded purple mulberries that were edible, but you had to watch out for the worms when you ate them. Its most important value to our family was that it was accessible to Mom or Dad when they needed switches to punish ornery kids. It furnished the "rods" that the Bible taught my parents "not to spare."

Our farm was three miles north and three and a half miles west of Erick, in western Oklahoma. It was located on the south bank of the north fork of the Red River. I was born there on a cold January day, 1926, the fourth child of my parents. In fact, I was the fourth baby born to the Sherman Rowland family in four years. The oldest was

James, followed in birth by Mary, Ruth and then me. Four years later another sister, Betty Jo, would be born, and our baby brother Rick arrived in four more years.

The limbs on the mulberry tree were slim and limber. My dad or mom could break one off, strip it of its leaves and apply it to our bottoms faster than you could say, "Jack Scat." Dad sometimes used his razor strap to punish us. It was made of leather and was about a foot and a half long, and was one and one-half inches wide. It always hung on the kitchen doorknob where it was handy, if needed. If I had my druthers, I'd by far druther had a licken' with the razor strap than with a mulberry switch.

There was a bench up against the big chicken house and a couple of chopping blocks to sit on when enjoying the mulberry tree's summer shade. When we had guests, the men gathered under the mulberry bush, sat on these amenities to discuss politics, religion and farming. The women stayed in the house cooking, washing dishes and discussing whatever women discussed.

I recollect the men discussing, and sometimes heatedly arguing about, everything from the work of the Holy Ghost to President Roosevelt's New Deal. The Democratic Party under his leadership had spawned a dozen or more programs to get the country through and out of the Great Depression that followed the stock market crash of 1929. There was the National Recovery Act, known as the NRA. Placards with a big blue eagle on them with NRA printed under it, were in store windows all over town. They were tacked on telephone poles and trees. Stickers with the same blue print were found on home and car windows. Then there was the Works Progress Administration, known as the WPA. There was the Agriculture Adjustment Act, AAA for short. There was the Emergency Banking Act designed to save the banks that were going belly-up every day. The Civilian Conservation Corps took young men from the poorest families away to camps to build mountain trails, Forest Service cabins and other work on all kinds of conservation projects. These boys were given two changes of clothes, shoes, board and room and a small monthly stipend for their work. They would stay away from home on these projects for up to six months at a time. It was known as the CCC. There was a dozen or more alphabet agencies that sprang up in an attempt to relieve the country's poverty. The Federal Relief Agency distributed food and clothing to the poor across the nation. Families lined up for blocks to take home free canned mutton and beef from Argentina, as well as flour, sugar, powdered milk, cheese and other surplus food stuff furnished by the government.

Lucky was the farmer who had shells for his gun to shoot an occasional rabbit, or dogs fast enough to catch one. Rabbit and chicken were the only fresh meats most farm families enjoyed in the summer months, because it was too hot to butcher a pig or a beef. We had no refrigeration, so, in the summer the meat would spoil in a matter of hours.

The NRA was declared unconstitutional by a decision of the Supreme Court in 1935. Dad said that if the Supreme Court would keep its nose out of the President's business the Depression would be over by 1937. Other agencies sprang up to take its place.

Farmers were paid to plow their crops under to reduce surpluses. They were even paid to kill and burn their cattle while people all across the country were nearly starving to death. Many fathers left the farming to their wives and sons, to go off and help build roads for a month or two at a time. One man with a team of horses and a wagon could make $26 a month on the WPA. In our family of eight, that was almost the only income we had many months. We did pay on our doctor bills by taking the doctor an occasional pound of butter or a dozen eggs. The money from a gallon of cream or a dozen eggs, sold at the creamery on Saturdays, was about the only other money most families had most of the year. We applied most of our produce money to our charge account at the grocery store, which helped keep the account open.

By 1935 the Depression was pervasive. A drought had settled in all across the Midwest. To add to the poverty in the Midwest, the dust storms had settled in. You could see a big dust storm coming five to ten miles away. The wind whipped up the dust from the topsoil from as far north as the Dakotas and down through Colorado, Nebraska, Kansas and Iowa. When a dust storm struck, you could hardly see your hand in front of your face. We tied wet handkerchiefs or rags over our mouths and noses to keep from suffocating. The storms, and the accompanying drought, began strangling the very life out of the land and out of the farmers.   At night the dust settled on the moist spots around your mouth, nose and eyes, leaving patches of caked-on clay by morning. The farmhouses were poorly built and none were sealed tight enough to keep the dust out. Most houses had no inner walls and we would tack construction paper on the inside in an attempt to slow the wind down as it blew through the cracks. Before we could afford the construction paper to tack on the inside of the walls, we glued newspaper on the walls and over the cracks to slow down the wind and the dust. We could read old news stories on these newspapers for months from our own walls.

On the mornings after a dust storm we would wake up to a half-inch of dust covering everything in the house. We would sweep up two or three tubs full of dust after every storm.

The banks that were still open were foreclosing on farm after farm. With farm foreclosures, the merchants could not collect their accounts, so they were forced to close their doors also.

About this time, family after family began to sell out. With the slim proceeds from their sales, they bought an old car or truck, threw a few sticks of furniture and a couple of mattresses on top, and headed for the Promised Land — California. Many vehicles broke down en-route and many of these migrants had little or no money for repairs. Some of our former neighbors were scattered from the state line of New Mexico along Route 66, all the way to the Promised Land.

My Uncle Earl and his family got as far as Lordsburg, New Mexico, when their truck broke down. It took them five more years to reach California. He died there from tuberculosis and was buried a long way from the family plot at Erick.

Our family did not know we were poor. Everybody else was in the same spot we were in. We accepted our lot, endured the hardships and hoped for better days. We were buying 160 acres of sandy farm-land on a contract with the bank. We also farmed 80 acres more that Dad inherited from Grandpa Rowland's estate. It was dry land farm-ing. If it didn't rain, you didn't have a crop. If you didn't have a crop, you couldn't pay off the crop loans or make the mortgage payments to the bank. After a couple of bad years the bank usually foreclosed.

We ate corn meal mush or oatmeal for breakfast. Cornbread and red beans were our staple lunch and dinner food. On occasion, it was supplemented with rabbit or chicken. The chicken was usually reserved for Sunday dinners. In the late fall we did butcher a pig or a calf to provide meat through the winter. Sometimes foodstuff was so scarce that our meals simply consisted of cornbread and a powdered milk mixture. Dad would sometimes pick up a soup bone at the butcher shop to throw into the beans to give it a bit of meat flavor.

The canned Argentine beef and mutton off the relief truck were added to the beans, and that helped. The mutton smelled so bad when it was cooking, you had to hold your nose, especially when you were eating it. The beef and mutton were gone long before the relief truck arrived in town the next month. The powdered milk, however, lasted all month. You could not mix it with water with any success. It was always lumpy and tasted nasty. We did learn that the hogs would eat it, so any left over at the end of the month went into the hog slop.

Since we had no type of refrigeration, the milk taken from our cows in the morning was blinky by noon and clabbered by suppertime during the summer months. We regularly drank clabbered milk at supper. We sprinkled it with a spoon full of sugar to make it go down easier. But, the sugar from the relief truck didn't last a whole month either, so we had to drink the clabbered milk without sugar at least half the time.

When my sister Ruth started to school at age six, I was left at home with nothing to do and my behavior sometimes caused a few more limbs to be broken off the mulberry tree. Mom and Dad decided that I could also do first grade work, so they enrolled me in the two-room Riverview School at age five. It was located a mile west and one mile south of our house. Even though I was a year younger than the other first graders, I was able to fit in and kept up with them in the books. Ruth did so well that she was promoted to the second grade before Thanksgiving.

At age eight, and entering the fourth grade, I recognized my individuality. My knowledge of my immediate world was pretty complete. I knew how to have fun, and I also knew the limits of acceptable behavior. Yet, there were plenty of used mulberry switches that would attest to my going beyond and testing the limits set for me. I wasn't the bravest boy in the fourth grade nor was I its biggest coward. In athletics I was average and in scholarship maybe a bit above average. You might say, "I was the best of the worst and the worst of the best" in most things.

It is in this fourth grade setting that my story begins. The year was 1934. It ends in 1936 when I was in the sixth grade.

I was eight and younger than anyone else in my fourth grade class. I was skinny but strong. I admit I was daring, but usually not too foolish. I understood my place in the pecking order of our family and on the school ground. I was willing to question authority if forced to by circumstances. Pulling tricks on my siblings, schoolmates and others broke the drabness of the poverty we were in. So, my mind was always on how to pull a good trick on somebody or anybody, young or old.

It was in the fourth grade that I came into my own, and the memories of that year and the next two are etched in my memory. One major event in my young life occurred during late summer school and just before a break of two months for cotton picking.

In Oklahoma, farmers tried to lay their crops by around July fourth. Around the middle of July, summer school started and lasted until Labor Day. One day in the summer session marked the date of one of my most memorable tricks. I didn't think I could ever top it, even if I lived to be a hundred. There was no one in our school, not even the meanest and most ornery eighth grader, who would have dared to do what Goober Powers and I did that day. Goober's name was really Paul, but we all called him Goober. He was a skinny kid and nearly a head taller than me. He was also a little stoop shouldered. The knees in all his pants or overalls had holes worn in them and the holes were frayed around the edges. Most of the boys had pants with holes in the knees but their mothers kept them pretty well patched most of the time. Goober's mom was a sick woman and bedfast. She couldn't do the patching on the pants and overalls in her family, so the holes in Goober's pants went unattended.

Nearly all the kids went barefooted from Easter until Halloween. We could only afford one pair of shoes a year and they had to last through the winter months.

This trick was the highlight of that school year. It is that experience and similar ones that I want to share. The story of *The Snake and My Teacher* is one of the most compelling stories in my young life.

CHAPTER 2
THE SNAKE AND MY TEACHER

Goober was one of my best friends. He was a year and a half older than me and in my grade. He was not the sharpest kid in school. He came by our house on the way to school every morning. He lived a mile east of us. The two of us usually paired off and walked to and from school together. We would spin yarns, dream dreams, and share thoughts. Sometimes, we would even plan innocent meanness on these trips to and from school. By the time we got to school each morning, there would be a string of kids stretched out at least a half mile in four directions on the two section line roads that intersected at the school. Almost everybody took the roads to school in order to join friends, or buddies, who came out of the farmhouses along the way. The average distance walked by every student, whether in the first grade or in the eighth, was about two miles. Some kids walked as many as three miles and a half. If you cut across the fields diagonally from our house to the school, you could save about a half-mile of walking, and you would arrive at school ten or fifteen minutes earlier than if you went around the fields by way of the roads. If you rushed, you could beat the rest of kids by a good twenty minutes. In fact, you could beat both of the teachers, as well as the kids, to the school grounds by cutting across.

One morning, Goober showed up early at our corner and suggested that we cut across the field to school and not mess around ahead or behind any other kids on the road. We did not have in mind any meanness. We just wanted to get to school first. We crawled through the barbed wire fence and headed toward the schoolhouse in a hurry. About halfway there, we ran across a bull snake about four feet long. Our first thought was to kill it, but there were no rocks or sticks to use in the middle of this field. We tormented this coiled up snake by throwing clods of soft dirt at it. But they did no damage even when we hit it. In a lull in our clod throwing, the snake decided to slither off and we followed it. It came upon a mole burrow and went right in. It stuck its head out of an exit hole in the dirt about three feet from where it had entered. There were about six inches of its tail still exposed where it entered the burrow.

Since we couldn't kill it, what else could we do to it? We simultaneously thought of catching it behind the head, carrying it to school alive and using it to scare the pants off the other kids. There was one major problem: which one of us was going to get close enough to grab the snake behind the head without getting bitten? Who had the strength to hold on to the snake all the way to school? We were both bare-footed and one of us was going to have to be brave enough to stomp down on the snake just behind its head. The other one was going to have to catch it right behind its head and carry it to school.

There was one story about one of our neighbors that caused us to pause. Every kid in the community knew about Mrs. Myrtle Hunter. She was missing half of her index finger on her right hand. The story was that she had reached for a fruit jar in their storm and fruit cellar and a bull snake, hidden behind the fruit jars, had latched on to her finger. In trying to sling the snake free of her hand, it was supposed to have pulled her finger off at the middle joint.

There were many nights that we went to our storm and fruit cellar when there was a bad storm and I'd lay there thinking of her finger. Tornadoes came through blowing houses and barns into the next county. We had one old chair in our cellar that mama seemed to always sit in with one of the babies during the storms. The rest of us sat, or laid, on a couple of quilts on the floor. When a storm was brewing, Daddy would wake us up from our sleep and tell us to run for the cellar. He made sure mama, the babies and all the older kids were safely in before he closed and chained down the door.

I never went to the cellar in the daytime to fetch a jar of food or during a storm at any time without thinking of Mrs. Hunter reaching for a jar and losing a finger. During a threatening tornado we didn't worry about shoes or clothes. We just ran for the cellar, sometimes half-naked.

When we were settled down I worried about a bull snake lingering behind a row of fruit jars just waiting to strike out and latch on to one of my toes. I wasn't worried about my fingers, because I wasn't going to reach out for a jar. But my toes were on a blanket or quilt on the dirt floor and I knew those snakes could crawl around.

Goober and I could count our toes. Neither was willing to volunteer to stomp on the snake with our bare feet in order to hold its head down, with the possibility of losing a toe. Nor was either of us too willing to grab the snake's neck just behind the head with our bare hands and in doing so, lose one of our fingers at the middle joint. This bull snake didn't move except to run its black tongue in and out of its mouth.

It was now time to piker somebody out. "If you don't stomp on its neck to hold it down you're a piker," I charged.

Goober replied, "If you don't, you're a fraidy cat."

We resolved the problem on which one would risk a toe first and which would then risk a finger later by going to the eeny, meeny, miney, moe method of selection. I began the litany, knowing in advance if I started with myself on the eeny, he would come out the loser. He innocently agreed to this process of elimination.

"Eeny, meeny, miney, moe, catch a rabbit by the toe, if he hollers make him pay, fifty hundred dollars every day. Birds fly east, birds fly west, birds fly over the coo-coo's nest. O u t spells out, you old dirty dish rag you."

Goober was it and we realized that time was important. He took a deep breath and jumped on the snake with both feet. He was more courageous than I was, but I couldn't let him know it. I wouldn't have done what he did. I would have changed plans about what to do with the snake. Now I was forced to do my part in order to save face. With great hesitance I reached down and grabbed the bull snake right behind its head. Goober happily jumped off and I pulled it out of the burrow. It quickly wrapped itself around my arm and I didn't dare let go of my grip.

Goober was jumping up and down and screaming, "We got it! We got it! We got it!" I was the one who had it and wasn't sure that I wanted it. We were both in a state of frenzy but it turned out that Goober had the best of our situation. He still had all his toes and I had a bull snake all right, but I couldn't let go of it. I was too afraid to even think about it. I didn't know where that snake would bite me first if I turned it loose and I certainly didn't want to lose a finger at its middle joint like Mrs. Hunter did.

We collected our wits and started running to the school grounds. Goober was carrying our lunches and books. I was running and choking the snake nearly to death. When we were about two hundred yards from the school grounds, the snake became limp and began to uncoil from around my arm.

Goober yelled, "You're killing it!" He then asked, "Who would be afraid of a dead snake?" "The snake ain't dead," was my reply.

I loosened my grip a little and the snake started to wiggle and waggle again. So far we had succeeded. We looked down the roads each way and there weren't any kids in a half mile. We walked to the front of the building and the doors were locked. The snake was getting heavier and heavier. My right hand and arm were about paralyzed from gripping it. We walked around the building and noticed the small door over an opening in the east schoolroom. The door had been placed there to put wood through and into a wood box when wood was used in the stoves for heating the building. We now used coal that was brought in big buckets from coal stored in the school's storm cellar. The door on the wood box was now nailed shut.

Every school and farmhouse had some kind of storm cellar to go along with it. Tornadoes were real threats, at least half the year. The school had the biggest and best one in the whole community. Its floor, walls and roof were made of concrete and steel.

All of a sudden scaring the kids wouldn't be nearly as much fun compared to our latest idea on what could be real, sure enough fun. Who cared about wood, coal or storm cellars, or scaring kids?

I asked Goober, "Why don't we put it in the teacher's desk?" He replied, "Because the school house is locked, stupid."

"Why don't we pry that door open and go in through the old wood box?" I asked.

He didn't think that was so stupid. He quickly retrieved an iron leg from an old broken desk and, in a jiffy, we had our entry. Goober had pried it open, I crawled in and he followed. He slid the top-drawer open on the right side of Mrs. Brook's desk. It was the one she kept her grade and attendance book in. I uncoiled the snake from around my arm and tried shoving it into the drawer. But it kept wiggling and trying to wrap itself around my numb arm again. Turning the snake loose now seemed riskier than any thing we had done with it so far. If I got it uncoiled and in the drawer, would it strike me before I got my hand out of the drawer? Would I lose a finger? These were real questions, and personally, they were real concerns.

Goober then helped me uncoil and stuff the snake in the drawer, and he pushed the drawer in until only my wrist was in the opening. I let go of the snake, yanked my hand out, and he slammed the drawer shut. We quickly exited the building, tacked the door shut and ran to the boys' toilet to hide. The school's toilets were two-holers with an L shaped shield wrapped in front to keep kids on the school ground from watching us as we did our business. They had been used ever since the schoolhouse was built, so they really did stink. Anytime anyone stayed longer than enough to do his business, we always knew something out of the ordinary was in the air. Boys usually gathered there to plan some meanness.

Goober and I waited until a dozen or so kids arrived before sauntering out one at a time on to the playground. Goober went out first, and I waited a few more minutes before leaving that stinking outhouse. But I didn't mind waiting in the stink this morning, knowing what was about to happen. The adrenaline was flowing. Goober and I were on a high that couldn't be described and it certainly couldn't be told.

In due time, the teachers arrived, and all the kids were having fun at a variety of games. The swings, see-saws, and the merry-go-round were busy. We stayed separated and watched the older boys play baseball. Neither Goober nor I could keep our minds on the game. When the first bell rang, we were always supposed to go to the toilet and then to the well for a last minute drink before entering the classroom. There we were seated as we waited for the second bell.

As we approached the well, Goober whispered in my ear, "I betcha a dollar that she'll pee in her pants."

I hoped not, but I did have other high expectations out of our well-executed plan. If we pulled it off and scared the teacher half to death, we knew we would have succeeded. If no one ever knew who did such a dastardly deed, we would have really succeeded. We would get off Scott free. Nothing we would ever do would be sweeter. We had pledged during our stay in that stinking dirty toilet that we would never tell anyone we did it, no matter what. We had already figured out that if the snake snapped off one of Mrs. Brook's fingers when she reached in for her grade book, we might wind up at the boy's reformatory in Pauls Valley. We had realized too late that this could be a serious trick — a sure enough serious trick.

The schoolroom was arranged so that we were seated in alphabetical order. Goober Powers sat directly in front of me. Our teacher, Mrs. Brooks, was a very wise woman. She had her desk at the back of the room and we all sat with our backs to her and facing the blackboard. This way it was impossible to know when she was watching you. Shooting spit wads and passing notes just didn't happen in Mrs. Brooks' room. And it was almost impossible to look at someone else's paper for answers without getting caught.

The first thing that happened every morning when books took up, and we were all at our desks, we stood and gave the Pledge of Allegiance to the United States flag. Then we recited the Lord's Prayer. Mrs. Brooks had a copy of the Bible on her desk from which she would then read a devotional passage. After this, we always heard the familiar sound of her sliding that top drawer on the right side of her desk open, reaching in to retrieve her grade book and then taking the roll.

Goober and I had an understanding that neither of us would turn around and gawk when and if she screamed. We were sure this would be a dead giveaway. The tension was so great that I could have screamed, even if I wasn't the one to reach in on a snake. I could hear the Bible close and I heard the teacher place it on the corner of the desk with a soft thud. Her chair squeaked a little as she turned to the right to open the top drawer. And, I would be able to remember the sounds that followed as long as I lived. The drawer made its usual squeak in opening. It was followed by a scream you could hear all the way to Filmore James' house, a half-mile away. Books tumbled to the floor. The girls screamed and the boys hollered. They all jumped to their feet and some circled her desk, at a safe distance, to see what had scared Mrs. Brooks — and them — half to death. But, two of the students didn't scream or jump to their feet to gawk. They kept their eyes glued on the spelling list on the blackboard with their backs to Mrs. Brooks.

The sound that immediately followed the teacher's scream was a loud thud. That thud was the drawer being slammed shut.

Almost immediately Miss Prock, the other teacher and half the kids from her schoolroom ran to the door of our room. They were poking their heads in with startled eyes. They were about as frightened as anyone was in our room. Unanswered questions ran through Goober's and my minds. We still didn't turn and gawk.

"Did she get bit?"

"Did the snake get out?"

"Would we be discovered as perpetrators of this heinous deed?"

Mrs. Brooks collected herself and instructed the students to return to their seats and sit down. She then raised her voice with an order that no army sergeant could have matched.

"Bob Rowland and Paul Powers, come to my desk immediately," she said. "Get the snake out of my top drawer and dispose of it!"

We went to her desk trembling with fear. How did she know we did it? The snake, that had been imprisoned in the drawer for over thirty minutes, had attempted to make its escape as soon as Mrs. Brooks opened the drawer a couple of inches. She reacted naturally by slamming the drawer shut, and in doing so, had cut the snake's head almost off. There was blood running down the front of the desk and into the drawer itself. Some had dripped on the floor.

We removed the snake, which was still wiggling a bit, but we knew it couldn't bite because its head was cut nearly off. We took it outside and threw it over the fence. We knew we were in trouble, but the joy of success that swelled up with pride in our chests was indescribable. The fear of what was to come did take some of the edge off that joy. But, the joy and pride of carrying off the trick far surpassed any punishment, unless you considered the possibility of spending a year in Pauls Valley. No one had ever pulled off such a prank in the history of Riverview School. Nor was it likely that that anyone ever would. We knew what was coming at lunch-time. But that didn't matter. We pumped some water at the well and washed the blood off our hands, took a bucket of water into the classroom to clean the teacher's desk and floor with.

Before we were to go to lunch, Mrs. Brooks announced that Bob and Paul were to return to the classroom as soon as they finished their lunches. She stayed inside to eat her lunch, then drove down to Filmore James' house to cut some switches. He had a row of mulberry trees in front of his house that produced switches as fine as those that grew on our tree at home. When she returned, she did not have a couple of switches, one for Goober and one for me. She had a dozen. If one broke, she had plenty in reserve. She was still mad enough to break some of them, too.

We went in and she had us bend across her desk, one at a time, right above that top drawer on the right hand side. She proceeded to punish us like she had never punished any students before. But, we deserved it. We had already sworn to each other that we would take our medicine like men and would not cry, no matter how hard she whipped us. By so doing, we could prove to each other and the other kids how tough we were.

As we were being whipped, there was a commotion on the south side of the building. I looked over and all the kids in school had their faces glued to the windows to watch us get our due. When it was over, as additional punishment, we were not permitted to go outside and play during the rest of the noon hour or at the afternoon recess.

Before recess, a dreaded fear began to set in on my mind. Daddy had a rule that he never violated or overlooked. If you get a whipping in school, you'll get one that night when you get home. There was no way that Dad would not find out about the snake with two sisters and one brother at school that day. Even if they did keep their yaps shut, the whole community couldn't and wouldn't keep their's shut.

When we finished the evening chores that included gathering the eggs, finding kindling to start the morning fire in the cook stove, chopping and splitting wood, slopping the hogs, feeding horses and mules, and milking the cows, Dad called me over to the big chicken house. He had a mulberry switch in his hand with the leaves stripped off. He told me that he was disappointed in my behavior. Then he kept his rule. I cried when he whipped me, because usually, the louder I cried, the shorter his whipping. At least it seemed so to me. So I bellowed like a lost calf. I didn't need to impress my brothers and sisters, or dad, how tough I was.

We gathered around the table that night to do our homework by the light of coal oil lamp. I kept watching dad and mom for some indication of forgiveness on their part. Dad and Mom did discuss this happening, the major event of the day, maybe of the school month or even the year. As they talked about it, I noted a particular glint in Dad's eyes, suggesting that he wasn't really all that mad and there was a suppressed smile on mama's face during the discussion. I decided that they really thought our trick was quite clever but just couldn't let on like they did. But I was also sure they thought that if I discovered of their admiration, it might encourage me to do even wilder things.

The snake incident didn't come up again until one Sunday morning when our whole family was in the wagon going to Sunday school and church at the schoolhouse. We were to have a sermon by a visiting preacher at both the morning service and the evening one. Mom and Dad wondered why he had been asked back, since they thought he was the dullest preacher they had ever heard. Mom commented, "It's going to be one long, boring day." James then spoke up, "Well, maybe Bob could catch a bull snake and turn it loose in the school house. That would liven things up." Mom, Dad and the rest of the family finally had their first laugh out of the snake incident. I sat in the back end of the wagon with my feet hanging over the end. I had a smile of real satisfaction on my face for the first time since Dad whipped me.

When school started again after Thanksgiving at the end of the cotton-picking season, there was to be a new addition to the sixth grade that would cause a continued commotion for a year. I could hardly wait to see her. Her reputation preceded her. She was supposed to be as pretty as a Hollywood starlet and to have all the spending money any kid would want.

CHAPTER THREE
TooWoo Tompson,
The School's Prettiest Girl

At age eight, as a boy who grew up on a farm, I didn't have to be taught about the birds and the bees. I knew about the birds, the bees and a whole lot more. There wasn't a boy in school who hadn't watched animals breeding and giving birth. We had heard and used every naughty word in the most profane farmer's vocabulary. The girls didn't use them, but the boys freely used the naughtiest words while in the company of other boys. From our earliest school age we not only knew the difference in boys and girls, but we were attracted to the girls. Each of us liked to claim one of them as our girlfriend. We said, "She was my girl, or your girl, or his girl." The boyfriends were always known as the girl's "feller." The prettiest girl in every room captured the attention of every boy in her class, and often had two or three boys vying for her attention. The prettiest girls in the whole school even had the older boys in the upper grades swooning over them, even if they were just fourth graders.

When school started in November for the long term, this girl from Oklahoma City enrolled in the sixth grade. Her name was TooWoo Tompson. TooWoo wasn't her real name, but that's what she liked to be called. She thought it gave her additional celebrity status. She had moved to the Riverview community to live with an aunt and uncle, George and Helen Martin. Her parents were deceased, one from sickness and the other from an accident. Her dad had bought a twenty-five-hundred dollar insurance policy on himself. TooWoo was an only child and the recipient of an annuity that paid her twenty dollars a month until she was eighteen years old. In our community, that was a fortune. Twenty-five hundred dollars would buy a one-hundred sixty-acre farm and leave enough over to put in a couple of crops.

TooWoo's aunt and uncle were her legal guardians, and they controlled her money. However, she could spend a lot of it any way she wished. She had a couple of dozen dresses, three nice coats, a dozen pair of shoes and any kind of toy she wanted. She had a bicycle but she couldn't ride it in our community because most of the roads were too sandy. She had a Tarzan and Jane metal lunch box with a Thermos jug in it. Everyone else brought their lunch to school wrapped in a newspaper or in a brown paper bag that they folded, took home and used over and over every day for one or two weeks. She had the money to attend every matinee at the Erick picture show house on Saturdays. Sometimes her aunt and uncle, who owned one of the few cars in the community, drove to Sayre, the county seat, to see the preview of next week's movie at midnight on Saturday. TooWoo had gone to see the scariest movie of the year, *King Kong*, twice. She had a whole shelf full of Big Little Books. They were stories about *Tarzan of the Apes*, *Dick Tracy*, *Tilly the Tollor* and other of our popular comic strip characters.

While all the other girls and boys in school had no more than one change of clothes, TooWoo couldn't count hers. Most of us had one set of clothes that we wore from Saturday through the next Friday. We then changed to the clean set to wear to town on Saturday and to Sunday school the next day. We wore these same clothes for the rest of the week. We usually changed clothes after our Friday night or

Saturday baths. The girls' dresses were made out of feed or flour sack material, as were most of the boys' shirts. Because everybody bought flour and feed, half the girls and women in the community had dresses and blouses with the very same colors and patterns from these sacks. In the winter, the boys wore long handle underwear. The girls all wore homemade flannel bloomers held up by rubber bands, cut from old inner tubes. They also wore long cotton stockings in the winter months, held up by rubber garters that also came from inner tubes.

TooWoo was different. She was also pretty. She was blond. She could afford to get a Shirley Temple permanent wave ever so often at the Erick Beauty Parlor. It was reported that she had taken tap dancing lessons in Oklahoma City and could tap dance about as well as Shirley Temple. All the girls knew that she wore silk panties. In our community, we called that "picking in tall cotton" or, "living high on the hog." The girls reported that some of her panties were even trimmed in lace. Such reports stirred the imaginations of the red-blooded country boys.

The boys were all struck on her. Every boy from the fourth grade to the eighth grade tried to get her attention. Every boy in the upper three grades would have given a right arm to be her "feller." But TooWoo was just too sophisticated to fall for these country boys. She was from the city, wasn't she? Moreover, after next year's crops were in and sold, she might move to California where all the movie stars lived. All the girls in the lower grades sought her attention and the older girls often competed for her friendship. At the same time, due to natural jealousy, some gladly stabbed her in the back.

One day one of my older cousins, Herman, dropped by school toward the end of the day. He had finished the eighth grade and spent six months in CCC camp in Colorado. He came home with two sets of olive green shirts and pants, as well as a fine pair of shoes. Most important, he had saved nearly every dime the government had paid him. He could afford to smoke ready-rolls like Camels and Chesterfields. Most of the farmers who smoked, smoked roll-your-own cigarettes with tobacco from Bull Durham sacks or Prince Albert cans. When we boys smoked, we smoked the cigarette butts found along the road discarded by those who rolled their own. If you found as many as four butts, you would have almost enough unused tobacco to roll yourself a real cigarette. But, you seldom found the butt of a ready-rolled cigarette on a country road. Farmers couldn't afford them.

On this afternoon Herman would tempt me with an offer to do another daring thing that I would later regret — at least somewhat. The other boys in the gang encouraged me to take his offer. It had a low temptation threshold for two reasons. Herman offered me a ready-rolled cigarette if I would run up behind TooWoo and yank her dress up so the boys could see her silk panties. That was the first reason. Secondly, I would get to see those panties and her bottom up close. We had just passed Filmore James' house and I was reminded of all the switches on those mulberry trees. But the temptation was great.

I told Herman, "Your offer isn't enough. It will be worth two Camel cigarettes for me to pull it off."

He grudgingly agreed, and I demanded that my buddy, Goober, hold the cigarettes for me in advance of my pulling off the stunt. When he had the cigarettes safely in his shirt pocket, the whole group of boys did double time until we caught up with the girls. We boys were walking together in a pack of about ten. I was walking about three steps ahead of the rest of the boys and TooWoo was lagging behind the bigger bunch of girls, with a couple of other sixth graders.

In my mind I had the plan laid out. When I got about three feet from TooWoo, I would lunge forward, grab her dress from the rear on both sides and yank it as high as I could. Then I'd take off for the fence next to the road, dive under it and cut across the field home. I would-n't worry about the cigarettes. I knew that Goober could be trusted to save the cigarettes for me until the next day.

The girls turned around noticing the approaching group of boys but had no idea what was on their minds. Ahead of the group, I slipped up behind TooWoo, lunged forward, grabbed her skirt with both hands and yanked it up. There before my eyes, and the eyes of nearly a dozen boys, was a pair of silk panties covering the bottom of the prettiest and richest girl in the whole county.

When TooWoo turned to see who the guilty party was, I had head-ed for the barbed wire fence by the road. I had not calculated two things in my plan to get away. The first was the goatheads and grass burrs growing between the ruts in the middle of the road and the fence. Nor, had I realized how fast TooWoo, being three years older than I, could run.

When my bare feet hit the goatheads and grass burrs, their stick-ers went through the soles of my bare feet nearly crippling me. The pain forced me to fall to my hands and knees and start crawling the final four yards to the fence. TooWoo was wearing black patent leather shoes and the stickers didn't slow her up at all. She caught me just as I started to dive under the bottom wire. She had that Tarzan and Jane metal lunch bucket in her hand and came down with it on the back of my head with all her might. It dazed me a bit but I knew that I couldn't slow down then. By the time she drew her hand back for the second blow, I was under the fence and scrambling back to my feet on the other side. I ran as fast as I could for about fifteen yards into Mr. James' cotton patch before I looked back. I was thankful that the fence stopped TooWoo's advance.

I turned around to survey the situation. The boys were doubled over in laughter and the girls were shaking their fists at them and me. I felt something warm on my neck. When I checked it out there was big knot on the back of my head about the size of a half of an English walnut. There was a gash across it about an inch long. Blood was coming out of it. I decided to walk parallel to the fence at a safe distance from the girls until we got to the next corner. There, a third of us would turn east and the rest would either go on north or turn west.

Before we reached the corner, I looked back. To both my sorrow and terror, I saw Mrs. Brook's new two-seated Plymouth coming down the road. Usually the students would step aside, and she would drive on by without slowing down. That wouldn't happen on this day. When her car got within fifty yards of the girls, they were standing in the middle of the road and had started flagging her down. The boys had already gone through the fences and were scattering in all directions. My sisters even joined in waving Mrs. Brooks down. What traitors! I'd be singing them a familiar song that night, "Tattle tail, tattle tail, hanging on a bull's tail." At least until Daddy got home.

Mrs. Brooks stopped the car and TooWoo ran over, put her foot on the running board and began tattling about what I had just done. I knew what I was in for during the next day at lunch and when I got home the next night. In fact, I worried that dad might just get his part over with tonight. My only hope of not getting a good switching was the fact that I had a bloody gash in my head. By the time we got home, the blood had dried where it ran down the back of my neck. So I went down to the horse tank and washed it off.

Of course the older boys and Herman were not punished. The boys weren't the ones who bribed me and Herman wasn't even going to school. So much for justice! I wondered all that night if those two ready-rolled cigarettes were worth the punishment I was going to have to endure.

The next morning Goober was late. I waited for ten minutes after my brother and sisters had left for school for him to show. I wanted to smoke one of the camels that morning, knowing I'd gladly share half of it with Goober. I finally left for school alone and really had to scoodaddle to catch up with the rest of the kids.

When I got to school, Goober was already there. He was slinking around the outhouse, so I knew something was up. I went down to it and asked for my ready-rolls. He stammered around like an egg-sucking dog. The son-of-a-gun finally admitted he had smoked one of the cigarettes behind their barn last night and the other one on the road to school this very morning. He had taken the other way to school instead of coming by our house, because he was afraid to face me and felt so guilty about smoking one of my cigarettes.

I was learning about loyalty and temptation.

Goober said, "I didn't think you would mind sharing one of the cigarettes in exchange for keeping them for you. So, I smoked that first one last night."

"Well where's the other one?" I demanded.

On the way to school, he decided to take the road south one-mile and then west one-mile to school to show off my last ready-roll to the kids who came from that direction to school. He didn't come by our house by going this way and he wouldn't have to face me so soon. After showing it, the boys encouraged him to share it with them. He thought that sharing my cigarette with them might garner him some special status in their eyes. He would deal with me later. But they thought no more of him after he shared my cigarette, than they did before. I knew they would not be any more loyal to Goober, or trustworthy, than Goober was to me. He had simply failed me. In addition to the knot and cut on the back of my head, I was going to have to take whippings from Mrs. Brooks and my dad. And I didn't get to take one puff on those two ready-rolls or even get to show off having them.

I had a knot on the back of my head with a slit in my scalp. Goober had the satisfaction of smoking one of my ready-rolls behind the barn and impressing some of the kids on the way to school by sharing my other one. I wanted to beat the dickens out of him right there and then. But, I decided that I needed some bigger cause to do that. So, I forgave him. He had been, and was still going to be, my best friend.

I accepted the whipping I received from Mrs. Brooks at noon and the one from my dad that same evening. I had decided it would be an even trade off, one whipping for each ready-rolled cigarette even if I didn't get one puff out of them. Weighing everything, I had decided that I may have gotten the best bargain after all. In the end, there was the satisfaction that I received by being recognized for being the only boy in school brave enough to do the deed all the boys wanted to do. I would have enjoyed puffing on those ready-rolls in front of the other boys, when most kids couldn't even find a short snipe to smoke. Of course, the best reward of all was that I got the closest and best peek of TooWoo's behind and silk panties of any of the boys in school.

TooWoo and her guardians did leave Oklahoma for California the next year. Their lease was up January 1. Most families who moved to other rented farms, in or out of our community, moved in January because that's when most leases expired. That way, those moving could get their new farms ready for the next year's crops.

We wouldn't have TooWoo around to gander at, be jealous of, or do things worse to any more. Two new families did move to the Riverview community in January. The children of one family, the Boyds that moved in, had attended Riverview School before. Everybody knew them. But the children of the other family that moved in, the Trubbels, would be thorns in James' and my sides for much of the school year. In fact, they had two boys who were bullies and they seemed determined to control everybody in Riverview School. The oldest was in the eighth grade and he set his sights to run the four upper grades. The youngest one, who was in the fourth grade, was determined to run the four lower grades. There was one big question, "Would there be any boys in the school who had the nerve to stand up to these two bullies?" Time would tell what kind of backbones the kids at Riverview School really had.

CHAPTER 4
WHOSE TURF WOULD IT BE?

When school started on January 2, 1934, we had these two new families in our community, the Trubbels and the Boyds. Four families had moved out. Two of them were heading for California.

The Boyds were returning after having moved away three years before. Their youngest girl had started in the first grade with Ruth and me. I was struck on her then and was still struck on her now that she had returned. The Boyds had two children who were still in grade school and two who went to high school in Erick. Etta Boyd was in the fourth grade and was still as pretty as a plum. She was smart as a dern whup and had nearly perfect penmanship. We quickly learned that you had to get a jump on her somehow to beat her in ciphering matches. You just couldn't beat her in spelling bees.

The Trubbels were new to the community but had other relatives who had lived among us before. Some of their relatives were known to be pretty tough and didn't mind getting into fights. It was also reported that they didn't mind using the threat of knives and other weapons if they got in a bind. In fact, it was rumored that one of their relatives had gone to prison at Granite or McAlester. Everybody knew that you had better keep a safe distance from any ex-convict or anyone connected to ex-convicts. They could be dangerous.

This wasn't the first experience the Rowlands had with the Trubbels. When Mr. Trubbel and my dad were in their late teens, they had a fight in town one Saturday afternoon over something. It turned out that my dad, who was pretty fair country boxer, had punched the living daylights out of Mr. Trubbel. In fact, the fight turned out so one-sided that Mr. Trubbel didn't show up in town again for a couple of months. My dad would not countenance bullies for a moment, then or now. This spirit would force decisions upon me that I really preferred not to make. But gaining the courage to make them would make my life better later on.

The newspapers of the era were filled with the exploits of gangsters like Baby Faced Nelson, John Dillinger and Pretty Boy Floyd. They would each die in hails of bullets from the guns of the FBI before the end of my fourth grade year. Pretty Boy Floyd was Oklahoma's own son. These gangsters' deeds of robbing banks and shooting lawmen brought anger to most people in our community. To other citizens, they were thought of as heroes. They took from the rich bankers and enjoyed spending their take on the good life that we all envied. Some Oklahoma citizens mourned when it was reported that Pretty Boy was shot. To them he was sort of a modern Robin Hood. I remember well that one of my cousins broke down in deep sobs when she heard the news of his death.

With Jimmy Trubbel and Etta Boyd as new additions to the fourth grade class, the mix of the pecking order in the class quickly changed. Sybil Hunter was no longer the prettiest girl in the lower four grades. Huck Jones, with all his charisma, could no longer use it to have his way in the classroom, playground or on the road home from school. Jimmy Trubbel would quickly ascend to the top dog spot in our room. Getting his approval was required on most things happening before books took up, during the noon hour, or during recesses. He dropped stories about life in the Hoxie School District they came from. He told of how tough he was and how many kids he had whipped, even those bigger than he was. And he was now the biggest kid in our room. He was also well muscled. Most of the boys in the room were skinny guys who always looked malnourished. It was not so with Jimmy. He was robust, able and ready to dominate others.

Huck Jones was the most popular boy in our classroom — maybe in the whole school. His parents didn't mind spending money on him. They bought him a fine painted pony and a saddle to go along with it. He was the only boy in school who wore cowboy boots. He had managed to be top dog in our classroom. This was due to his sense of humor, his ability to manipulate, and the fact that he had more things than any of the rest of us had, including a Red Ryder BB gun.

When school started after New Year's, I began shining up to Etta Boyd immediately. I would pass notes to her at recess. And to show my daring, I'd do so even after books took up. She reciprocated with notes that showed that she was interested, even if it didn't seem that she was as interested in me as I was in her. By February, I had staked out my claim on her and even spent my last dime, earned from last fall's cotton picking, to buy her a store bought valentine for Valentine's Day. Most of the kids exchanged valentines that were cut out of colored construction paper furnished by the school. Any messages were written on with pencils or Crayolas. That was the best Jimmy could come up with. Going into March I figured I still had the advantage with Etta. It was during this month that everything would change.

Jimmy came up with an old cheap ring that had a ruby colored glass setting in it. I wondered who he had stolen it from, but I wouldn't wonder it out loud. I told Goober that it was just one step above the kind you got out of a Cracker Jack box. One morning I noticed that

Etta was wearing that ring. I handed her a note at recess asking where she got it. At noon she passed me a note saying, "You know where I got it, silly." The fact that she called me silly hurt enough, but the fact that she would wear Jimmy's ugly old ring hurt even more. It didn't take long for the story to get around to Jimmy that I not only thought his ring was ugly, but that I also resented Etta wearing it. That meant that I was probably going to be in trouble with Jimmy, something I didn't want at all.

Every evening after school my first chore was going to the river bottom, rounding up our cows and driving them to the cow lot next to our barn for their nightly milking. One evening I had just reached the river to look for the cows when I noticed Huck Jones on his painted horse about a quarter of a mile up the river. Someone was on the back of the saddle riding with him. I was happy to see Huck. I waved my arms and shouted to get his attention. He turned the horse toward me and it loped in my direction. When he got about a hundred yards from me, I knew I had made a big mistake. Jimmy Trubbel was the one riding behind the saddle. I had no one to protect me or defend me —not my big brother James, not the teacher, nor my parents. I was alone and it was obvious that Huck had hitched up with Jimmy and he wouldn't be of any help to me either. I couldn't run. I would have to do my best to act like we were all bosom buddies. Maybe then Jimmy wouldn't jump on me about Etta Boyd.

Huck stopped his horse right in front of me and Jimmy piled off just as if it had been planned. He walked right up to me and stuck his finger in my face.

"You are jealous of me because Etta is wearing my ring aren't you?"

"No I'm not, and I don't know what you are talking about," I lied, as meekly as possible.

"Yes you are and yes you do," he charged.

"No I'm not and I don't either," I pleaded.

"She's not your girl. So get it straight, she's my girl and she's wearing my ring."

"I know that and it's OK with me," I gladly granted him.

"I don't need your permission," he said.

"I know that," I said.

"You wasted your money on that valentine too," he informed me.

That really hurt. Etta must have shown him that fancy valentine and let him know that it didn't mean anything to her. Otherwise he wouldn't have said that. Would she really make fun of my store-bought valentine to Jimmy? I wondered.

Before I could finish my wondering, Jimmy said, "We can settle this right here and now."

"But," I protested, "we don't have anything to settle."

"Yes we do. Put your dukes up and we'll settle it fair and square. Whoever wins the fight will have Etta as his girl," said Jimmy.

I didn't want to fight Jimmy and I had lost all my interest in Etta. I certainly wasn't going to put my fists up and invite him to punch the living daylights out of me. So I just stood there submissively with my hands in my overall pockets. If I moved one hand, I knew that he would feel justified in throwing the first blow.

"You're nothing but a chicken and a fraidy cat," he taunted.

If he had asked me to admit that, I would have, gladly. I would have done nearly anything to get him back on that horse and ride away. But, he wasn't going away.

I glanced from him up to Huck for some sympathy, help, or anything. But I noted a big smile on Huck's face that suggested he was enjoying this confrontation, maybe more than Jimmy was.

Jimmy could wait no longer to establish his dominance over me. He threw a punch that landed on my chest and I was so thankful to him that he didn't hit me in the face that I nearly expressed it. I did fall to the ground as if he had really knocked me down. He demanded that I get up and fight. I gladly complied with his order to get up, but I still would not agree to the fight.

He punched me in the chest again, and again I sprawled backward on the ground. He grabbed me this time by my overalls' bib, yanked me to my feet and punched me in the chest again. And to the ground I was happy to fall again. He stood over me and glowered. He warned me that if there were a next time, he would bloody my nose and black both my eyes.

In the meantime, Huck Jones was enjoying the scene immensely. In fact, he was laughing so hard that he nearly tumbled out of his saddle. Jimmy told me to "git" and I "got." When I looked back, they were riding up the river toward Jimmy's house.

I rounded up the cattle and drove them home. I couldn't tell a soul. Even though I was the youngest kid in our class, to be afraid of anybody in my class was sort of a disgrace. To let anybody bully me wasn't Rowland-like. They stood their ground and they fought for what they believed was right. The only problem, I was the only Rowland who had to face Jimmy Trubbel every day of the week and sometimes on Saturday. The rest of the Rowlands didn't.

Etta kept wearing Jimmy's ring and I kept as much distance from her and him as possible. There would be no more notes, no more winks and certainly no more shining up to Etta.

Spring came, and with it warm weather came. Usually our whole family would climb into the wagon and go to town on Saturdays. Saturdays had always been great days. Everybody did their weekly shopping, visited old friends, and waited until four o'clock for the merchant's drawing before heading for home. With every dollar a family spent on groceries, tools, feed and seed all week, the family received a free ticket for the weekly drawing an Saturdays. At four o'clock, right in the middle of Main Street on someone's wagon bed, three tickets were drawn out of a barrel for the prizes. The first ticket got a prize of one dollar. The next ticket was a prize of five dollars. The final ticket was a prize of ten dollars. This weekly drawing not only attracted people to our town, but it created loyalty to the merchants who sponsored it.

It was on one of these Saturdays that James and Dad were down by the barn harnessing the horses in preparation for our weekly trip to town. I looked up and saw the Trubbel wagon coming down the road. I ran into the house and watched through the window as it passed by. Mr. Trubbel and Earl were riding in the wagon seat and Jimmy was sitting in the back with his feet dangling down. By this time Earl had pretty well taken over the upper grades at Riverview School and Jimmy had totally taken over the lower grades. Going to town meant that I would have to face Jimmy in the town sometime that day and do his bidding.

The last time we met in town on the same Saturday, he caught me in a back alley and told me to go into the variety store and steal him a five-cent Butterfinger. He ordered Goober to help shield me from the eyes of the clerk so I wouldn't get caught. We were to do the stealing while he waited outside to watch out for Elmer Renner, the town marshal.

He had it pretty well worked out. And, it was all to his advantage. He would stand guard outside the store on the sidewalk while Goober and I did the stealing. If we were caught he could just saunter off down the sidewalk while we were getting arrested. Who could prove that he had anything to do with it? If the marshal had shown up and caught us doing the stealing, only Goober and I would be in trouble. We would spend the night in the town pokey and Jimmy would go home and sleep in his own bed.

I stole the Butterfinger as commanded by slipping it into my bib pocket. Goober and I moved on to the toy counter and then out of the store and around to the back alley behind the Dixie Store. Jimmy came from the other direction. When he met us, he demanded, "Let me have it!" I slipped it to him and he broke a small piece off the end of the candy bar for Goober and I to share while he ate the biggest part. It wasn't fair, but neither of us wanted to have Jimmy beat us up for refusing to accept his decision on what was fair in the division of the candy bar we stole for him and risked going to jail for.

So on that Saturday morning I started getting a pain in the pit of my stomach. I informed mama that I didn't feel good, as she was dressing my little baby brother Rick. She suggested I'd feel better by the time we got to town, but I wasn't so sure. In my heart of hearts I knew that with Jimmy Trubbel in town I couldn't feel any better, and I could feel a lot worse.

When Dad and James came up to the house with the team of horses hitched to the wagon, my stomach was really hurting. I was almost in tears. Daddy didn't really care whether I went to town or not. But he did wonder if I was too sick to stay home by myself. He told Mama to give me dose of Castor Oil, and ordered me stick around the house until the family got back home, if I was going to stay home. I had the choice of getting better quickly and going into town to face Jimmy or taking a dose of Castor Oil and staying home. I hated Castor Oil almost as much as I hated Jimmy Trubbel. Castor Oil or Epson Salts were the country remedies for every thing from a sore throat to constipation. I easily chose the Castor Oil and Dad's "Stick around the house" order over facing Jimmy.

Mom gave me teaspoon full of Castor Oil and it nearly made me throw up my breakfast. It was awful. Then she picked up the baby, went out and climbed up in the wagon seat next to Dad. Dad picked up the check lines and started the team out to the road and toward town. He hollered back, "Don't build a fire and don't get into any trouble." I wouldn't need a fire, and how in the world could I get into any trouble all by myself? Who did he think he was kidding?

I watched the wagon go over the hill and disappear from sight. As I went into the house, it dawned on me that I would be there alone for the next six or seven hours. About the only book in the house was the Bible and neither we, nor anyone else in the community, had a radio. We did have last month's copy of the *Capper's Farmer*. It was a farm magazine we subscribed to. I gleaned all I wanted from it in about thirty minutes. Then I was bored again. I could go rabbit hunting but there were no shells for our 22 rifle or the 12 gauge shotgun. Moreover, there was a rule that I couldn't hunt with a gun by myself either, even if we had shells. If I went hunting, I'd have to use the dogs and go alone. But that wouldn't really be much fun.

After awhile, I thought of going down to Pete Morris's house to see if Mrs. Morris would let Joe and David come down to our house to play. I had seen Pete and three of their children pass by in their wagon just a few minutes behind the Trubbels. David and Joe weren't with them. David was a year older than I, but in the fourth grade. Joe was my age and in the third grade. The Morrises had nine kids and always had one on the way.

Dad had said once, "If Pete Morris knew as much about growing cotton as he did about growing kids, he would be wealthy." Mom laughed at his observation and remarked, "You are one to talk."

I went down to the Morris's place and they were in the middle of the Saturday laundry. The boys were keeping a supply of wood handy in order to keep the water in the big iron wash pot boiling. The girls were switching off between scrubbing clothes on a wash board, wrenching and hanging the clean sheets, pillow cases, shirts, dresses, overalls, long handles and bloomers on the clothesline. Mrs. Morris was standing, pregnant, in the doorway of their house, doing the ironing.

After a little talk, I asked David and Joe if they would like to come down to our house and play. I told them that no one was home but me. We could climb up, then slide or roll down our big hay and fodder stacks, and, we could play Tarzan in the barn. We could even take the dogs rabbit hunting if they wanted to. I even offered to share the rabbits if we caught more than one. They had an old skinny dog but it was so slow. Dad said it couldn't run fast enough to catch a cold, let alone a rabbit.

On that basis, I asked Mrs. Morris if they could come to our house to play and then go hunting with the dogs. She said it would be OK if we didn't take a gun. But, before we left, we were to make sure there was enough wood chopped to finish the laundry. So we chopped up a big pile of wood and said goodbye. As we walked by the door on our way to the road, Mrs. Morris said, "Now don't get into any trouble, you hear?" We assured her we wouldn't and we were off to an afternoon of fun.

When we got to my place, we went to the barn and swung on the rafters. We bellowed like Tarzan and imagined that we were in a thick jungle facing apes and gorillas. We made elephant calls and chased tigers and lions. When we had enough of that, we went out and climbed the big hay and fodder stacks. Then we would slide or roll off of them with great delight.

After this play we were dusty, hot and thirsty. We went to the house to rest and get a drink of water. There were three biscuits left over from breakfast in a pan on the shelf above the cook stove. I had planned to eat them with plum jelly for lunch. But, a decision on what to have for lunch would have to come later, if it came at all.

My dad dipped snuff and always had a big brown bottle of Honest Snuff on the top of our cabinet right beside the Hershey's Cocoa can. Every morning he would fill a little snuff can out of the bottle to dip from during the day. He carried it in his shirt pocket where it always wore a hole through, even before the shirt wore out. He wouldn't let his kids dip snuff or use any other kind of tobacco. He said we would have his OK to use tobacco when we were twenty-one years of age if we wanted to then. That didn't keep us from finding out what was so enjoyable about dipping snuff, chewing tobacco or smoking. James and I tried them all.

James and I had already found out about smoking and dipping. Our exposure to dipping came one Sunday afternoon when our family was visiting the Whitelys. We had gone to their house for dinner after Sunday school. James and I walked home early to do the chores and the Whitely boys, Roy and Harrel Ray, went with us. That brown bottle of snuff was a constant temptation when we were alone and it became too great a temptation with the Whitely boys there with us. We took the bottle down and put a half-teaspoon of snuff under our lower lips. We pranced around like big shots with our lips pooching out. The snuff started the saliva flowing and that caused us to start spitting. From my observation, people dipped snuff in order to spit a lot. The snuff stains remained on their teeth and in the corner of their mouths long after they quit spitting. Every snuff dipper and tobacco chewer had a coffee can around to spit in. Some would put ashes in the bottom of it to absorb the spit and some would just have a can half-full of dirty smelly snuff or chewing tobacco spit. Dad always put ashes in his can. Both kinds of spit cans were just about as nasty as our outdoor toilets.

Marion Dobson, even though he was a teetotaler when it came to drinking any kind of booze, didn't find it sinful to use tobacco in any form. He mostly dipped snuff or chewed Day's Work chewing tobacco. His wife, Edna, was a dipper and always carried around a can of snuff. She also had her own spit can, too. Daddy would trade off between dipping snuff and chewing tobacco. He liked Brown Mule chewing tobacco over Day's Work. He said it was sweeter. No kind of tobacco tasted sweet to me.

My Aunt Maud used snuff, as did a fourth of the women in the community. But she didn't spoon a bunch of it up and put it under her lower lip like everyone else did. She made little brushes out of Devils' Claws, a weed that grew wild. After they bloomed and dried up, the big plants left a bunch of ugly shells with four sharp claws about three inches long on them. She would chew the blunt end of a claw into a brush, dip it in the snuff can and brush the snuff on her teeth and gums. She then used the claw end to hang it on the lapel of her dress. When she wanted more snuff, she would put the brush end in her mouth, get it wet with spit and repeated the process.

I never could understand why anyone could kiss a man or a woman whose mouth was so dirty and stained with snuff. Since I wasn't planning to do much kissing, at least not very soon, I was willing to enter the world of snuff dippers myself. I guess I would have made an exception to kissing a snuff dipper if she was Etta Boyd or Sybil Hunter.

Our journey into the world of snuff dipping that Sunday afternoon with the Whitely boys lasted only about fifteen minutes. In that length of time, we had swallowed a pretty fair amount of the snuff. Of course the nicotine from this ground-up tobacco was poisonous. The four of us, having developed no tolerance for tobacco poison, started getting sick. Before long we were getting dizzy and started throwing up. I didn't have to be told again to wait until I was twenty-one years old about using this form of tobacco.

On this Saturday afternoon, I looked up at that brown bottle of snuff and wondered if David and Joe would like to try some. They turned down my offer. Then I wondered if snuff would affect dogs like it did humans. I knew we couldn't tempt the dogs into taking a dip of it. Using the three biscuits, however, was another matter. Every time we had some leftovers to feed the dogs, all you had to do was to call them and throw it out. They would catch anything that wasn't liquid before it hit the ground. So, we split the biscuits open and put a teaspoon full of snuff in each biscuit.

We called the three dogs up and pitched a biscuit to each one. They grabbed the biscuits in mid-air and gulped them down. Then they stared at us begging for more. Their begging wouldn't last long. In about five minutes they started rubbing their heads and jaws in the grass. Then they started rolling around in it. In few more minutes, they started throwing up. They staggered and they gagged. We laughed and we hollered.

The three dogs were nothing alike. The oldest, Peg, was an Airdale and had been given to James when he was about two years old. Shep was a Shepherd dog and was a lot better at chasing rabbits than herding animals. We got him out of litter of pups that came from a bitch dog owned by the Meffords. We were given tacit approval by Mama and Daddy to use the word, bitch, when we were talking about a female dog, but were forbidden to use it in any other context. Any other use would constitute cussing. The third dog was Snowball. We got her by accident.

One day I was coming home from school by myself when I was in the third grade. The reason I was coming home by myself, was that the fourth through the eighth grade kids were taking achievement tests. So I, along with the other little kids, was let out early.

Between school and our house was a corrugated culvert under the road, about eighteen inches in diameter. We had just gone through a big dust storm and the culvert was almost half full of dirt. As I walked over it, I heard a faint whine. I stopped and heard it again. We never crawled into a culvert because we feared that a rattlesnake might be hiding in it, so I kept my distance from the end and peered in. It was dark and the whining grew louder as soon as I called out to whatever was in there. I was afraid it might be an opossum, and heaven forbid that it would turn out to be a skunk. I could see something moving in the darkness but could not make out what it was. But I was sure it wasn't a rattlesnake and I couldn't smell any skunk odor.

I crawled up to the end of the culvert and when my eyes adjusted to the darkness, I could make out a little gray dog. It refused to come to my calls or whistles. I called and it whined. My compassion finally gave me the courage to crawl in, rattlesnake or no rattlesnake. I caught the puppy and dragged it out into the sunlight. It was almost a ball of dirt. The dust had settled around its eyes as they watered, and the dust had caked over them so thick that the dog could not even see. I rushed home with the dog and mama put it in the dishpan. And with warm water cleaned up its fur and its eyes. When she rinsed it, it turned out to be the cutest, fluffiest little white dog you could ever imagine.

Mama said somebody must have abandoned it there, rather than knocking it in the head, because they couldn't afford to feed it. I was proud that I had saved the puppy and I immediately named her Snowball.

When the rest of the kids returned from school that day, they fell in love with this friendly little mutt that had been abandoned by some cruel farmer. When Daddy came home, he was not happy to see the dog at all. In fact he exclaimed, "Where in the hell did that mutt come from? It can't stay around here." I explained how the dog got here, and he still wasn't impressed. I knew he wasn't going to knock it in the head, but I was afraid he would take it town the next Saturday and try to give it away.

Snowball was such a playful and happy little dog, that she won Daddy's heart. In fact, she was the first dog that he would allow to stay in the house. The other two could not even come into the house, even during blizzards. She didn't know it, but like TooWoo Tompson, she was going to California some day.

But that afternoon, when David, Joe and I were not to get into any trouble, was not over. Little did I realize that I would get myself into the kind of trouble, before the day was over, that it would give me a moniker that I would be called by as long as we lived in that community. It seemed destined to happen.

CHAPTER 5
I WANT TO BE A BARBER

When we finished laughing at the antics of the drunken dogs, we realized there would be no hunting with them that day. And there would be no sharing of rabbits either.

It so happened that my dad was a fairly good country barber. Nearly every Sunday we would go home with some other family for dinner after Sunday school and church. Or some family would come to our house for dinner. It was usually a chicken dinner and about the only time we had chicken. When we went to someone else's house, Dad would often take along his barber tools. He had half of a bed sheet. It served two purposes. It was used to keep hair off the clothes of the ones getting the haircuts and for wrapping his barber tools in after the barbering was over. These tools consisted of a set of hand clippers, a straight razor, a long narrow barber's comb and a pair of barber's scissors. He would place these tools on the wagon seat between him and mama on the Sundays we were going to eat at somebody else's house. He also had another tool, a razor strap that always hung on the inside kitchen doorknob, except when he was barbering under the mulberry tree. It was used primarily for sharpening his straight razor and for punishing children in the evenings when it was too late to go out and break switches off our mulberry tree. When we were home, he stored this package of tools above the door in the kitchen, wrapped in the half-bed sheet. Using any of these for any other purpose was a no-no.

During cotton picking season, on some Saturdays, Dad worked at the town barbershop while James and I took a wagon full of cotton to the gin. This was about the only time in the year that farm families had enough money in their pockets to pay for their haircuts. The cost of a haircut was twenty-five cents. Dad kept ten cents and the owner of the barbershop got fifteen cents from each haircut. He could cut up to six heads an hour on a busy day. So he made nearly four extra dollars every Saturday that he had a chance to barber during the cotton picking season. That was real money and paid for lots of groceries.

As David, Joe and I were running out of things to talk about or do, I glanced up and noticed that package of barber tools above the door. I then noticed the razor strap swinging from the kitchen doorknob and then looked at David and Joe's heads.

"You guys need a haircut," I announced. And, they did.

"So?" They responded together.

"Well, I'll cut it for you and won't charge you anything," I offered.

"You can't cut hair," they responded.

"Oh yes I can. I cut James' hair every other time and Dad's, too. I even shave Dad's neck with the straight razor after I cut his hair," I lied. Then I added, "You guys look like sheep dogs."

That judgment on their looks seemed to work. They began to consider my offer. David was smart enough though to say, "If you cut anybody's hair, you'll have to cut Joe's hair first."

I finally persuaded Joe to give me a chance to prove that I was a barber. I clinched the deal with this argument. "You know your dad can't afford to have you get a haircut in town. So, this is the same as getting a quarter for nothing."

Joe reluctantly agreed to my offer of a free hair cut. I took the barber kit down and we marched down to the shade of the mulberry tree.
For a barber chair, Dad always stacked the two chopping blocks on
top of each other. I stacked the blocks and patted the top surface of
the upper one, indicating that Joe was to take his seat there. He got up
on the top block and I proceeded to wrap that half-sheet around him.
When I pinned it around his neck, I nearly stuck the safety pin into his
gullet. If I had, my barber career would have been cut short. But, by
pinning the sheet on loosely, I did not endanger him further, or my
career.   It didn't look like he had had a comb in his hair for a week
or more. I tried to get that little tapered comb through his hair and
failed. When I pulled it through his matted hair, Joe would yell. If I
did it gently, I got nowhere. So I canceled the combing and picked up
the clippers. I clipped away at his sideburns and at the back of his
neck. I then took the scissors and trimmed around and above his ears.
I ran my fingers through his hair and trimmed off the hair that was
sticking up between my fingers like I'd seen my dad do a hundred
times. The more I clipped, trimmed and tried to comb his hair the
worse the job looked. I ran the clippers over and around his ears, but
nothing would even out between the two sides. The clipped hair on
the back of his head never merged in length or in line with the hair on
the sides of his head.

When I decided I couldn't do much more, I unhooked the safety
pin, took the sheet off and shook it out. I then invited him to go into
the house and check it out in the mirror on Mom's dresser. David took
a look at it and said, "It looks gawdawful." Joe went into the house
and came right out saying he thought it looked gawdawful, too.
I admitted it was bad and blamed it on the dull scissors.

"Dad was supposed to have them sharpened in town last week,
but, he forgot to," I explained. My explanation didn't satisfy Joe. He
complained some more.

I said, "What did you expect for nothing? You got a lot more than you paid for." Joe was still not satisfied with my reasons or the haircut, where upon I offered to fix the haircut by giving him a butch. "That would be better than what I've got now," Joe said. "Well, get back on the chopping block," I ordered. Joe obeyed and I proceeded to clip his whole head right down to the skull. When I finished, his head looked worse than before. There were dips, scoops, and ridges that looked plumb awful. Even I admitted that.

"Go in and look at it now and tell me what you think," I suggested. He came out and told me that I was just getting it worse instead of better. I admitted that it did look pretty bad.

I countered with a proposition that he couldn't turn down. "If I shave it, it will be as smooth as your head, and you can't have it any smoother or more even than that. That way it'll all grow out even, just like the Lord shaped your head." I assured him again that I had shaved my dad's neck lots of times and he was none the worse for it. And, I didn't bat an eye when I told him. With reluctance, he finally agreed. Now it was necessary to break one of the rules dad had laid down for me before going to town. If you were going to shave somebody, you had to have hot water. To have hot water you had to start a fire. So I started a fire and heated a teakettle full of water.

I took a chair down to the mulberry tree and sat a wash pan full of hot water on it. I soaked a towel and wrapped it around Joe's head. As his hair soaked, I hung Dad's razor strap on a nail in the trunk of the mulberry tree. The nail had been driven there just for that very purpose. Then I took Dad's straight razor and stropped it back and forth in an attempt to let both boys know that I knew what I was doing and that I could do it. When I had sharpened it, I took Dad's shaving mug and whipped up a good lather.

Joe sat very still when I took the towel off and lathered his head. He sat even more still when I approached with him with the straight razor. I started the shave him from the front of his head to the back. My first stroke shaved a strip of hair about one and half inches long and a half-inch wide right down the middle of his scalp. It was there that I hit a bump and cut him. He flinched and accused me of cutting him. I assured him that it was just a little nick and he had nothing to worry about. I had something to worry about though. That nick was really bleeding. I wrung the towel out and blotted the blood up. I also made sure he didn't see any blood. I started another furrow in his hair next to the one I had just made. I hit another knot on his scalp and it began bleeding. The third try made its nick about an inch back. All three nicks were bleeding. My, I didn't realize how much a head could bleed from what I described as, and which seemed to be, just small nicks. I guess I had forgotten about the amount of blood I lost from the slit that TooWoo Tompson had made in my head with her Tarzan and Jane lunch bucket.

With little success on top of his head, the towel folded and placed there to soak up the blood, I moved to the back of his neck. The skin there gave a little and I was making great progress all across his neck. That is, until I reached the bony spots on the back of his head. There I cut him again.

David was leaning against the old mulberry tree playing mumblety-peg with an old pocketknife that had two blades. One of the blades was broken in half so he wasn't having the best of luck sticking it in the ground. He looked at Joe's head that was now bent forward so I could shave the back of his neck. He spotted the blood soaking through the towel. He screamed, "Datgum you Bob, stop! You're killing him!" Where upon Joe reached up and grabbed the blood soaked towel. When he saw the amount of blood that had oozed from his scalp he squealed like a stuck hog. He yanked the sheet off, sending the safety pin holding it flying under the big chicken house. He started for the road and his mama. I ran and grabbed him by the waist trying to convince him that he really wasn't hurt. Badly hurt or not, he had seen the blood, and he was hurt enough not to stay around me and that razor. He was going home if he could get away. I was pleading with him to let me finish the job. I promised I wouldn't cut him again. He was squalling louder than a turpentined cat and begging me to let him go. David stepped in and demanded that I let him go. I knew I couldn't control 'em both, and together they might beat me up.

I let Joe go and he headed down the road screaming for his mama like someone was killing him. David was running to keep up with him and I was trailing along behind, begging them to stop and come back. When we got about two hundred yards from their gate, Mrs. Morris heard Joe's bellowing and ran out to meet him. A half dozen brothers and sisters followed her. This was when I realized that I was really out-numbered, and I had no idea how they would take it. I turned tail and headed for home. I cleaned up the barber tools and put them away. I washed the towel out and hung it on the clothesline to dry.

When the family returned from town, I had the cows in the cow lot, wood chopped and the water buckets on the kitchen shelf full. I had nothing to report except that the Castor Oil must have worked, because I was feeling fine.

The whole Morris family seldom came as family to Sunday school at the schoolhouse. There were just too many kids to get ready and they could hardly all get in one wagon anyway. Mrs. Morris and some of the children came some of the time, but Pete seldom did. He would hitch up one of their two teams of mules to the wagon so she and the children could go. But he preferred not to listen to the Bible lessons and the singing. He claimed he couldn't sing anyway. He didn't like the Bible lessons because he couldn't read all that well. The way the teacher conducted the adult class was for each person to read a verse in the passage being studied when it came their turn. After you read your verse, you were supposed to explain what it meant. Since Pete couldn't really read well, it embarrassed him to have to. And, he reasoned, if you can't read the verse, how can you explain it? So, why go to Sunday school to be embarrassed?

Of all the Sundays I was hoping that Mr. Morris and his family would choose to forsake the assembly of the Lord's people, it was today. I was even praying, "Lord, don't let the Morrises come today."

As various families began arriving for church in their wagons, I kept a lookout for the Morris family's team of mules and wagon. On a good Sunday, there would be at least fifteen wagons tied up to the fence that ran in front of the school grounds. I kept looking down the road north. To my utter dismay the Morris wagon came into view. There were Pete and Joe sitting on the wagon seat and a half dozen more kids riding in the wagon's bed.

I high tailed it into the schoolhouse where the women and girls had gathered. They were already singing church songs. On a typical Sunday, the women would sing three or four songs before the men threw down and stomped their cigarette butts out or spit out their cuds of tobacco to join the women for services. I grabbed a Sunday school card and started working on my memory verse. The windows were open to let the air circulate through the building, so you could hear the conversations outside about as well as those on the inside.

I turned my head toward a window to observe the gate into the school grounds. Mr. Morris and Joe entered together, with the other kids trailing behind. I then heard my dad ask, "What in the wide world happened to Joe's head, Pete? Did he get it caught in a mowing machine?" All the men and boys turned to see what Dad was talking about and they began laughing. Pete answered, "No, it looks like Bob turned barber yesterday while we were all in town." Everybody out in the front of the schoolhouse then had a big laugh as they sort of inspected Joe's head.

After one more song, the men and boys began sauntering into the schoolhouse. When Joe entered, he had three furrows in his scalp where the hair was shaved off. They were running from the front of his hairline back an inch to an inch and a half. The back of his neck was shaved off pretty smoothly until the shaving reached the bony spots on the back of his head. At the end of the each furrow, and where the shaving stopped on the Joe's head, red scabs were forming. The women then began laughing. My barbering job almost looked scary. The whole congregation then began to laugh together and Joe was so humiliated that he started to cry. I felt guilty and wanted to go over to console him. But, I couldn't because it was my fault that he was crying.

I didn't get much out the Bible class or the services that morning. I spent that time dreading what was going to happen to me when we got home. Nothing was said on the way home about Joe's haircut. Nobody in the family seemed to even want to bring the subject up. They knew that Dad was still stewing over my deed. He was so angry they thought they might have to witness me getting a whipping, with the horsewhip, before we even got home. But, he was a whole lot angrier that had I used his barber tools than what happened to Joe's head.

By the time we got home, baby Rick was asleep in Mom's arms. Daddy stepped down from the wagon and took Rick from Mom and carried him into the house. Over his shoulder he said, "James, you and Bob put the wagon and horses away." I thought maybe Dad was seeing a little humor in what I had done and that I might get off Scott free. After all, Joe sure got big laughs when the men first saw him at Sunday school, and Dad had laughed the hardest of anybody.

But this wasn't to be the case. Just as James and I had unharnessed the horses and started to the house, Dad met us at the mulberry tree. And, a couple of limbs later my barber career came to an end. Dad warned me, "Don't you ever get caught using my barber tools for any-thing again young man. Or, dat gum it, it will be worse. You are just too full of piss and vinegar for your own good," he charged.

Coming to the end of my barber career didn't end the barber tale. The next morning as Goober and I joined a group of other kids at the corner, they were waiting for me. In unison they yelled out, "Here comes Barber Bob, hee, hee, hee. He'll cut your head off, for free, free, free." A year later people were still singing that ditty and getting fun out of it at my expense. But at our house it was no laughing matter.

One Saturday morning, the next September, Daddy was laid up with a bad back and couldn't go to town to barber to make our gro-cery money. The family was discussing the problem at the breakfast table. Mary came up with the perfect solution. "Maybe Bob could go to town and take Dad's place in the barber shop while James takes the cotton to the gin." Everyone rolled in laughter.

The jokes about Barber Bob didn't stop until we forsook that com-munity and left for California. Nor did it appear that Jimmy Trubbel's bullying me would stop either. But, my dad would have a solution for that problem and he was determined that I use it. My problem: was I more afraid of my dad than I was of Jimmy Trubbel. That test would come shortly.

CHAPTER 6
WHO WILL CHALLENGE THE BULLIES?

In the spring, a young man's fancy turns to baseball. So it was at Riverview School. Our school ground barely had enough room for one regular sized baseball field. If the lower grades wanted to play baseball, they had to climb through the fence and play on one laid out in Joe Van's pasture behind the boys' toilet. The school's baseball field was always occupied by the kids in the upper four grades. Some of the girls were about as good at baseball as were some of the boys. My sister Mary was one of them. She could also fight, wrestle and race competitively with any boy her age.

By baseball time that year, Earl Trubbel had established himself as the man in control of recess and noon happenings by those in the upper grades at school. He also bluffed his way to being top dog in the groups walking to and from school. Jimmy was a spitting image of him, not only in looks and build, but in demeanor, too. Just about anybody in school, except the teachers, would agree that the two Trubbels had taken charge of everything at Riverview School but the classrooms. The teachers even seemed to be reluctant to intervene in squabbles, except in the worst kind of bullying.

My brother James didn't cotton to Earl any more than I cottoned to Jimmy. There was one difference in the two relationships, James wasn't really afraid of Earl, while Jimmy terrorized me. The Trubbels were always bragging about their tough relatives and the kids they had beaten up over at Hoxie. Their stories didn't impress James. James wasn't afraid to call Earl a windbag to his face. This caused Earl to seek a variety ways to show James he didn't have to respect him and that he was still the boss of the upper grades.

President Roosevelt's relief program under the New Deal had sent supplemental food to the schools in a hot lunch program. The free food was mostly soup and salt crackers. It also included cocoa for a hot drink. Most of us still brought a biscuit sandwich or two made with a piece of ham, bacon or fried eggs. Sometimes we would just have a cold buttered biscuit sprinkled with sugar. It served as sort of a dessert. The idea of a sandwich made from sliced store-bought bread with bologna or cheese was about as foreign to us as tacos. Most of us had eaten neither.

TooWoo Tompson had been the only girl in school to have bologna sandwiches made of real store-bought light bread. She also had an apple or an orange to go along with them. For dessert, her aunt put a couple of chocolate drops or a couple of one-cent candy bars like Baby Ruths or Butterfingers. We all envied TooWoo, and wished we could bring that kind of a lunch to school. On occasion she would share some of her goodies with someone who didn't seem to be part of her admiration society. A penny candy bar or half of a bologna sandwich could buy lots of admiration and friendship.

One Friday night, Daddy came home from the WPA work camp, and he had a half loaf of store-bought bread left over from batching in the camp. We children wanted to eat it right there and then, but Mama said that we would save it. We wondered for what?

There were just enough slices of the bread for each of us to take a store-bought sliced bread sandwich in our lunch on Monday. We would show everyone that the Rowlands had arrived uptown, even if it were just for one Monday. I was certain, however, that we would be unable to show them our uptown arrival on future days. But we had our fifteen minutes of fame.

At school we usually sat around on that concrete storm and coal cellar to eat our lunches and soup while drinking our hot cocoa. On that Monday, I removed my store-bought bread sandwich from my brown paper bag and spent ten minutes nibbling on it. I wanted to make sure every kid in school saw my sandwich, as did my sisters. We were the last kids to the playground after that lunch break.

At noon, after washing our hands, the lunch line always formed while we waiting to get our cup of hot cocoa or soup furnished free by the United States government. It was here that Earl would find out if he really had a hold on the upper grades. As we lined up, I was right behind James and we were about tenth and eleventh in line. Earl washed his hands, walked up to Jewel Comstock, who was fifth in line, and just butted in the line in front of her. Jewel was kind of struck on Earl, so she wasn't objecting. But, datgum it, James did.
He ordered, "Earl to go to the back of the line."

Since bullies don't really know what fair means, or that decent folk take their turns, Earl ignored James' order to go to the back of the line. When he ignored James' second order, which he yelled at him that time, James walked up and yanked him out of the line by the straps of his overalls. Everyone knew that a fight was beginning. The line broke up as the girls scattered and the boys formed a circle around James and Earl.

Earl doubled up his fists and circled James. Quick as flash, James shot a right fist out and bloodied Earl's nose. And, quicker than a flash, he punched him the second time in the mouth. The second blow split Earl's upper lip wide open and the blood gushed out of it. So much blood was spurting out of his nose, you would think that it was broken. The blood splattered everywhere. He was bleeding like a stuck hog. The girls were getting sick and the boys were looking on in amazement. Earl was bleeding and crying. Mrs. Brooks ran out to see what the big commotion was all about. She took Earl over the water pump and told Jenks Dobson to start pumping. The cold water from the well slowed Earl's bleeding from his nose and upper lip. But his shirt had blood all over it and his upper lip swelled up as big as crab apple and was about as red as one. With that split lip, he didn't enjoy his hot cocoa for the next few days.

The kids argued that James was only trying to make everyone abide by the rules and that he did not deserve punishment. After lunch, though, the two were brought into the schoolhouse for the teachers to decide their punishment. They both lost. Earl had no business breaking into the line and raising his fists. James had no business yanking him out of line, because that was the teacher's job. This fight, that was not a fight, brought on another trip by the teacher down to Filmore James' mulberry trees.

After supper that night, Dad called James away from the table and down to the big chicken house and gave him a switching. No one around the table would have voted for that punishment, had we had a vote. Peeking through the back screen door, I noted that it wasn't a hard switching because Dad really thought James did the right thing. In fact, I knew Dad did not whip James for punching Earl in the face. He knew Earl deserved that. He gave James a whipping because he got one in school. He wouldn't violate his own rule.

It took a few days for Earl's lip to heal and a few more for the school to fully realize what had happened to the power mix in the upper grades. James had become a hero to most of the kids in both rooms. Earl was subdued and wasn't nearly as brash as he had been. He no longer thought that he needed to be the center of attention in everything or have the answer to every question. He no longer acted like a smart-aleck either — at least around James.

This was not so in the lower grades. Jimmy was king of the mountain and no one had entertained the faintest notion of challenging him. He decided who would play what positions on his baseball team and if and when they would bat when his side was up. There was no questioning of, or challenges to, his authority. If you complained, he would punish you by making you play a position you didn't like or withholding your right to bat when it was your turn. If you complained to the teachers, he could and would make your life miserable in other ways. If you tattled on him to the teachers, he, and those he controlled, would gather to point their fingers at you while singing, "Tattle tale, tattle tale, hanging on a bull's tail" over and over again. There wasn't any escape from Jimmy's domination and the humiliation he caused.

When the baseball season got well underway, there was a game before school, at the recesses and during the noon hour. Jimmy and Huck Jones always chose up sides. Jimmy usually picked me, not because I was so good at baseball, but just so he could let me know who was boss. I simply couldn't get out from under him anywhere. If our team was behind and it was my turn to bat, he didn't mind grabbing the bat and forcing me to the bottom of the order. No one thought this was fair, but no one dared complain. If we were three or four runs ahead, his charity showed by allowing all players to have their turns at bat, even me.

My sister, Ruth, observed it and her sense of fairness caused her to speak up for me one day. "It's Bob's turn to bat," she yelled. But, her request for fairness fell on Jimmy's deaf ears. I'd druther that she had just keep her yap shut about fairness if it involved Jimmy and me. That night she spilled the beans on how unfair Jimmy was treating me in the baseball games. Dad would not for a minute have me go tattling to the teacher. However, he did have a very practical solution to the problem. He told me, "The next time he tries to take the bat away from you, when it's your turn to bat, punch him in the nose and bloody it. While you are at it, hit him again and bust his lip, like James did to Earl. That will fix him." That sounded easy at the supper table two miles away from the school. But it wouldn't sound easy at all standing in front of Jimmy Trubbel at home plate. That would be especially true if he had already taken the bat away from me and had it in his own hands.

Dad put a clincher on his advice with this order, "Anytime Jimmy takes the bat away from you and denies your right to bat when it's your turn, you punch him. If you don't, you'll get a licking from me at night." I still didn't know who to fear the most — Dad or Jimmy. The only thing different about the choice was that usually, after a switching, Dad took me in his arms after my crying stopped and assured me he loved me. Jimmy would just glare at me with anger in his eyes.

The next night at supper, Dad asked me if Jimmy had denied me the right to bat again. As I was stammering around trying to come up with an answer that would satisfy him, Ruth blurted out, "Yes sir, he did it again today." After supper we went to the mulberry tree but he didn't give me a switching. Dad told me to come over and sit down beside him on that bench by the big chicken house. He put his arm around me and said he really didn't want to give me a switching, but that I had to stand up for myself because no one else was going to. He hugged me close and told me that Jimmy was really a coward, as were all bullies. It was easy for him to say that, because he didn't have to face the guy every day, who, in my way of judging, was not even close to being a coward.

Then he gave me a plan of action that was more terrifying to try to execute than punching Jimmy in the face. He knew that Jimmy was stronger than I was, and that in a fair fight he'd probably beat the dickens out of me. So he gave me permission to level the playing field, so to speak.

He said, "If Jimmy tries to take away the bat again, as he approaches you, threaten to bop him on the head with the bat, that'll do the trick." He assured me that it would work. "Even if Mrs. Brooks suspends you for a week it will still be worth it," he assured me further.

I went to bed imagining that I not only threatened to bop Jimmy on the head, but that I bopped him on the head with the bat and had him on his knees in front of me, pleading to me, Bob Rowland, for mercy. Moreover, I would probably have Dad's blessings. That was a good feeling to go to sleep on.

That vision was a great morale booster. But the vision diminished considerably as I was milking old Sway the next morning before breakfast. Every minute that passed I was brought closer to the O K Corral for a showdown.

I was caught between two choices — I could continue to take the humiliation Jimmy heaped upon me in front of the other kids, and face Dad every night. Or I could muster up the courage to use the bat and threaten to bop Jimmy on the head with it. If it worked he would know he wasn't my boss any more.

On the road to school the next morning, I was glad to report to Goober what Dad had told me to do. But by now, I wasn't going to just threaten Jimmy with the bat, I was going to use it on his punk'in head. I had moved my action to another level. Jimmy would have knot on his head as big as a goose egg after I bopped him. Goober was impressed. He kept saying, "Wow! Wow! Wow!"

He didn't have that kind of courage, and in his gut, he doubted that I did. Yet, he knew that such an action might just put Jimmy in his place forever. After a few more wows, he asked, "But what if you kill him?" I'm not sure that I cared that much, but I knew if I decided to hit him, I wasn't going to hit him that hard. In my mind, I would hit him just hard enough to serve notice that I would not be intimidated again. And Jimmy would never know what I might resort to the next time he tried to keep me in my place, as he saw my place. Even if I knocked him out and I was arrested for it, I didn't think they would keep me locked up in Pauls Valley forever. I even imagined that even if I were sent there, it would be a pretty fair trade off.

At my age, I still did not understand how quickly loyalties could change. I did not know how fear alone could cause someone you trusted to abandon you. But I was about to learn.

At recess, Jimmy didn't call for the choosing up sides to play baseball. In fact, he announced there was to be no game. He ordered Taylor Comstock to leave the bat and the ball in the schoolroom.

He had summoned me to come down behind the boys' toilet where he would conduct a hearing. He sent Goober, to fetch me. Goober came over to the swings where I was standing and watching the girls swing. He asked me to go down to the toilet with him. I assumed he wanted to tell me something in private. When we walked around to the back of the toilet, there stood Jimmy and Taylor.

Taylor was small and chunky in stature. It seemed that he always had a cold with snot running down to his upper lip. When it wasn't running, he always had one finger in his nose, picking it. Like most of us, he usually wore hand-me-down clothes and shoes. By spring our shoes often had holes in the soles or were split out between the sole and the upper part. When there was snow on the ground, our dads, or moms, would wrap tow sacks around our feet to keep them warm and the snow out as we walked to school.

Jimmy had summoned Taylor as a witness of how he would treat anybody who challenged his authority. He had summoned us down to let all of us know that he would beat the living daylights out of anyone who dared hit him over the head with the baseball bat. Moreover, he'd do me like his cousin had done to a kid that hit him with a bat. He said his cousin had taken the bat away, knocked the kid down, held him down, and rubbed his face in the gravel until the skin came off. Then he turned him over and let the blood from his head wound run in the kid's face. That scene he painted terrified Goober, Taylor and me. It would've probably terrified sixth grade boys too. He informed me that Goober had told him that he better look out because I was going to bust his head open with the baseball bat if he tried to keep me from batting today.

Anger swelled up in my breast. Paul Powers was a no good suck-egg-dog. We had no more than arrived at school and he had gone lickedy-split to tell Jimmy what I was going to do. No one knew it outside our family and I knew they wouldn't betray me. So Paul was a traitor. I wouldn't even call him Goober.

I said, "I did not say that. It's a lie."

Paul declared, "Yes you did, just this morning."

"I did not! You are a lair, Paul Powers."

"Yes you did!" said Paul.

"No I didn't!" I said.

Jimmy had heard enough. "One of you is a liar."

Court was being held and he was the prosecutor and the judge. Taylor was the witness. But, he would have sworn to the teachers on his grandmother's grave to have never been to this meeting if Jimmy told him to.

Right then and there he was firming up his total control over the three of us. My plan had been discovered, due to the act of a traitor. I looked at Paul with total disdain and contempt, about the way Jimmy usually looked at most of us, most of the time.

I claimed that Goober was lying and that I had not told him that. Goober declared that I had told him that, and that I was lying by denying it. Jimmy had the solution. He pronounced his judgment.

"Bob, you are going to have to whip Goober on the way home from school today to punish him for lying about you. Goober you are going to have to whip Bob on the way from school today because he has accused you of lying about him."

King Solomon could not have done a better job. The fight planned by Jimmy was whispered throughout the school all day. The gladiators would meet and fight to the finish in the old buffalo wallow in Mr. Ward's pasture. Everyone who wanted to see the fight could come. The Ward pasture wasn't by the road the teachers went home on, so the fight would not be stopped until one of us had cried, "Calf rope" or started crying. But our code stated that you would never say, "Calf rope" or cry unless you were nearly killed.

Everyone in the community knew where the buffalo wallow was. It had been used for fights to settle school ground fusses every since the schoolhouse was built. It was there in the days of the Indians. The buffalo used to wallow in it to get dirt and mud on their hides to keep the flies off. It was about thirty-five feet wide and three to four feet deep. When a fight was on, the kids would sit around on the edge of the wallow with their legs hanging off. The wallow was a ring and all the kids had ringside seats. Everybody who went home on the north and west roads was there. Some even doubled back from the south road to watch the fight.

Joe Louis had just won his big fight over Jack Kracken, and was going on to become the greatest heavyweight of all time. We had walked all the way to the Davis ranch to listen to it on the radio. There must have been fifty people in the Davis' yard listening to the Brown Bomber win.

With more than half of the school kids watching, this was going to be almost as important a fight to one of us as that one was for Joe in Detroit. Hopefully, one of us was going to leave the buffalo wallow on the good side of Jimmy Trubbel, and I'd fight like the devil to make sure I was the one.

When everyone was seated Jimmy told the students that we were there to settle the matter between Goober and me. He said one of us had lied to him, and this fight would determine who had had done the lying.

The fight started as we circled each other. We jabbed, punched and threw haymakers. Some landed but many didn't. I don't think Goober really wanted to hurt me, but I wanted to hurt him for his betrayal. If one of us had recanted, and admitted to having lied, then only one of us would be in a fight. But, it would be a fight between Jimmy and the one who confessed. If Goober would say he lied, the fight would be between him and Jimmy. If I had admitted to making plans to bop him over the head with a baseball bat, then I would be fighting Jimmy. The choice of fighting each other, versus fighting Jimmy, was never even considered by any stretch of either of our imaginations. We would rather pound the daylights out of each other five times than to face Jimmy just once.

I finally bloodied Goober's nose and he began to cry in the third round. I had suffered enough blows myself and would have cried if I thought Jimmy would have called the fight off early. He did call it off and warned both of us never to lie to him again or we would be down in the buffalo wallow with him the next time.

As Goober and I walked home that last mile to my house, we made peace. He admitted that he told on me to curry favor with Jimmy. He also claimed that he did it to keep me out of Pauls Valley reformatory because I might have killed Jimmy. That being the case, all was forgiven and we shook hands on it.

That night, I decided that I had enough humiliation and terrorizing by Jimmy Trubbel. If my brother wasn't afraid of Earl, then it was time for me not to be afraid of Jimmy. I wouldn't put it off. For my sake, Goober's sake and the sake of all the kids in the lower four grades, this was going to end. Tomorrow there would a change in the order of command at Riverview School. I was determined to do what Dad said I ought to do. I'd bop Jimmy Trubbel over the head with the baseball bat and stop him from bullying me around. At the least, I would threaten to bop him over the head.

That night the fight was talked about around the supper table. Again, Dad encouraged me to stand up to the bully and use the bat to scare him, if I had to. He said it would take some backbone. And he knew I had it, if I'd just use it.

I walked to school with Goober the next day and I told him that the plan was on. I was resolved to stand up to this big bully and see if my dad was right, that all bullies are really cowards.

As soon as we finished eating lunch and washing out our cocoa cups, Jimmy said, "Let's play baseball," as he started through the fence to the diamond in the Joe Van's pasture. He was carrying the bat and the ball. Sure enough, he selected me to play on his team. I was selected as his fifth choice. I came up to bat first in the second inning. I went over and picked up the bat and Jimmy told me that Taylor was up to bat.

"No it's my time to bat," I protested, trying to cover my considerable fear.

"Taylor was chosen sixth. I was chosen fifth, so it's my time to bat," I claimed.

"Give Taylor the bat!" he ordered.

Instead of handing the bat to Taylor, as I had always done before, I walked up to the plate with the bat firmly gripped in my hands. I looked straight into Jimmy's eyes, defying him. He knew I was defying him. I rotated the bat above my head and then pointed it right at Jimmy's head. I then looked at him with eyes filled with total defiance.

I then turned and shouted to Huck Jones, "Pitch the ball."

Huck was pitching for the other side. He always pitched. He pitched because that's the way the teams were always divided up. Jimmy ran everything on one team, but allowed Huck to be his lieutenant and run the other team for him. Huck always chose sides, so he always got to pitch. No one questioned how it was done. No one protested Jimmy's pitching for one team and Huck pitching for the other. Pitchers were big shots and big shots got to pitch.

This time Huck didn't even spread his feet. He was making no attempt to pitch the ball. He didn't even look at me, but he did keep his eyes on Jimmy. Suddenly it was now or never for Jimmy to maintain his grip on half of the school.

He commanded, "I said, give Taylor the bat!"

I did not even glance toward Taylor, let alone offer him the bat. But I did shout to Huck, "I said, pitch the ball." Taylor was more nervous than Huck was. He kept looking for Jimmy to make his move on me. But he saw my defiance of Jimmy and declined to take one move toward me or at taking the bat. Everybody knew about my threat to bop Jimmy over the head, and with me having the bat in my hands, Jimmy wasn't going to make a single move toward the plate to get it, nor was he.

The longer the standoff, the greater my courage and determination grew. Daddy's words came back, "All bullies are cowards." What seemed an eternity was probably less than a minute. By now, I was determined to bop Jimmy over the head with that bat if necessary even if dad hadn't told me to go that far. If he didn't go down, I was prepared to give him a second shot with it. I pointed the bat at Jimmy's head again. His eyes shifted from me and he turned his head toward the schoolhouse. No teacher was even looking our way. There was no one to come to his aid if I decked him. He was now convinced that I was going to deck him.

"I dare you to try taking this bat away from me," I taunted. I was amazed that I could even talk.

"Come on and get it right between the eyes tough guy," I threatened. I waved the bat above my head and said, "Come on tough guy. Let's see who bleeds in whose face."

I didn't know where I got that kind of courage. It was kind of like an "out of the body" experience. My heart was beating a hundred miles a minute.

No more orders came out of Jimmy's mouth, and he made no moves but nervous ones. Everybody could see that he was getting shifty eyed, backing down and chickening out. My how quickly the winds change. Yesterday, I'd have done anything Jimmy told me to do, and in the way he told me to do it. Today, I was defying him and rescinding his orders.

I then ordered Huck to pitch the ball and he spread his feet and delivered the ball. He didn't try to brush me back like he often did. Suddenly, there seemed to be a respect for me that I had sought all year. I got a hit and was on base. Taylor didn't need Jimmy to tell him to bat next. He picked up the bat and walked to the plate without even getting a nod from Jimmy. Instead of standing around giving orders, Jimmy suddenly needed to go to the outhouse and didn't come out until the first bell rang. He missed his next time to bat, and I even took his place pitching. On any day before this happened, we would have all waited for him to do his business in the outhouse before we went on with the game.

He came out of the outhouse as we passed it on our way to the school well. Emboldened by the events at hand and the bat I was carrying, I sarcastically asked him, "What's the matter Jimmy, are you constipated?" He wasn't constipated. In fact, Goober answered my question. He was brave now that somebody had finally challenged Jimmy. "No, he's not constipated, Bob. You just scared the crap out of him." Everybody in hearing distance laughed. They were now brave enough to laugh at Jimmy Trubbel! What a change! What courage we had mustered in those fifteen minutes!

The next morning Goober and I were on the way to school and saw Jimmy waiting for us down at the corner. At first, fear came over me, but I was not going to let it control me again. I walked proudly right up the corner and to Jimmy. James and I had slain the two Goliaths at Riverview School and we didn't even use a sling, a rock or a baseball bat. Jimmy was humble and amicable. For the first time, I chose the one of the sides up for a ball game at recess and Goober got to choose one of the sides at noon.

Finally, James and I were out of bully trouble, but we were each about to get in the kind of trouble that we should have avoided.

CHAPTER 7
GRAND THEFT

There was a group of would-be and real cowboys in our community who decided that they should have a rodeo occasionally. The rodeos were to be held down in the bottom of the North Fork of the Red River. There were lots of range cattle that freely roamed the river bottom. They were owned by a myriad of ranchers and farmers. Their brands were the only way to tell them apart. The cattle were pretty wild and that made them pretty good stock for the rodeo. There was a large cattle pen near the Red Bluff watering hole with a loading chute on it. It hadn't taken too much work to convert the pen into a usable rodeo corral. Nearly every guy under thirty-five years of age in the district thought that he was a pretty fair cowboy.

They got the word out about the rodeo around Erick, and had a bunch of cowboys sign up to ride, rope and bulldog. They even included a contest in wild cow milking. Those who couldn't ride bulls, rope calves or bulldog steers, could team up with someone who could rope and try their hand at wild cow milking. The way that worked, a cow, which was dry, was chased out into the arena and a cowboy would rope her. While she was bucking and tugging at the rope, his partner would run out to the cow, grab a tit and try to get enough moisture or milk out of it to show up in a Coke bottle. The cowboys that brought moisture in his Coke bottle to the judges in the shortest amount of time, won.

They scheduled the first rodeo on a Sunday afternoon in early April, just before Easter. On Saturday afternoon they rounded up a bunch of cattle most likely to be fine buckers and ran them into a holding pen next to the bigger corral. They didn't have bronc riding because all the horses had to pull plows the next week and most of them were broke to ride anyway. After Sunday school and church, many of the young men took off for Red Bluff and the rodeo. Most of the men went home after church because it was considered a sin, by many adults, to go to rodeos on the Sabbath. Boys, however, were somewhat exempt from the Sabbath laws.

James, our cousin LeeRoy, and I left the schoolhouse as soon as the last prayer was said, and headed for the rodeo on foot, Sabbath or no Sabbath. En route, we stopped at our house just long enough to grab a biscuit sandwich to eat on the way.

We got to the rodeo in plenty of time to see the whole thing. There were no admission charges and everybody was there for the fun of participating or to watch. Some of the cattle didn't buck very well, and some not at all. But there were enough that did to make it fun. The calf roping and bull dogging were the best events. After the wild cow milking and the last steers were ridden, we started home. We were about four miles from Uncle Earl's house and five miles from ours. There were few roads across the river bottom, so we could save lots of walking by cutting diagonally across the bottom from Red Bluff to Uncle Earl's house.

About halfway across the river bottom, we spotted a donkey grazing next to a water hole. LeeRoy wondered if we could catch it. That seemed to be a good suggestion. We surrounded the donkey and it wasn't too hard to catch. The question after catching it was, "What are we going to do with it?" We couldn't take it home. We didn't even own it, or know who did. But, maybe could we take it home? LeeRoy had a greater imagination when it came to things like this than James and me.

Uncle Earl's clan was different than our side of the family. It was more daring than our side in walking a fine line in regard to the law. The boys were tough as boots. They were known as the best fist fighters in our community and maybe in all of Beckham County. They drank, and it was reported they sometimes even made and sold bootleg whiskey. At the least, I knew they made and consumed quite a bit of home-brewed beer.

In order to understand how James, LeeRoy and I ended up the way we did that Sunday, you would have to know a little more about Uncle Earl's family and how it ticked.

There were four boys in the family. They were a year or two apart in age. There were also four girls, Eilene, Elsie, Doris and Marlene. Elsie died at about age 7. She was the first dead person I had ever seen. We went to Uncle Earl's house for the funeral and most of the neighbors attended. A Baptist preacher from town came to preach the funeral. He assured us that we would all see Elsie again in heaven, and that was comforting to me. He described heaven right out of the Bible — God's throne, the pearly gates, the streets of gold and all. I wondered if they could play Annie Over up there like we did when Elsie was alive. I doubted it, because I figured God's temple would be just too high to throw the ball over.

She was in a small casket, dressed in a pretty white dress and appeared to be just sleeping. I had played Annie Over with her a couple of weeks before. I was saddened when they put her casket in a wagon and started off to the cemetery. I would never play Annie Over or Hide and Seek with her again.

The deaths of babies and young children were common at that

time. Dyphtheria, chicken pox, small pox and influenza took the lives of both young and old. Seldom did all the children born in a family reach maturity.

Uncle Earl's two middle boys, Herman and Roger, competed in everything. The oldest boy was Darrel. LeeRoy was the youngest and the same age as my brother James. Darrel, the oldest, and Roger, the number three boy, were pretty good buddies. This meant that Herman was always at a disadvantage in any competition. When Darrel and Roger teamed up, they could overpower Herman and force him to do their will if their parents were not at home to intervene. If they needed any extra help, LeeRoy was always there to support the winners. Darrel and Roger together, of course, were always the winners. Therefore, it was usually three against one.

One day Herman and Roger got into a bad fist fight. Herman was the victor and went to house to take a nap afterwards. Roger would have his revenge, though. While Herman was asleep, Roger stood a beer bottle, the long neck down, on the heating stove. When it got really hot, he sneaked up on Herman and shoved that red-hot bottle's mouth to his cheek. He was branded for life. Roger ran while Herman screamed and tried to get something to relieve the pain. Roger returned in time for supper but Herman's cheek was too raw and sore to resume their battle. But, a couple of days, later Roger was napping after lunch and Herman got his revenge. He returned the favor by branding him on his cheek with the same bottle. They would go to their graves with those circles branded on their cheeks.

Herman was born with a little extension on his tailbone. In fact, it was a little tail. His brothers started calling him possom, Poss for short, because it looked like the tip of an opossum's tail. By the time he started to school everyone in the community called him, "Poss." One day Darrel and Roger had a dispute with Herman, and Herman was losing. He called the two some pretty dirty names. Uncle Earl and Aunt Merle weren't at home, so Darrel and Roger were free and able to take Herman down and tie him up. They decided to jerk down his pants and cut his tail off. They used a straight razor to do the operation.

When the news reached our house, Dad said they could have paralyzed him. But he was no worse for the surgery. He would, however, be known as Poss for the rest of his youth.

On another occasion, Darrel and Roger took the shotgun to go rabbit hunting, and Herman wanted to go along. He claimed the shells belonged to him as much as they belonged to the other two. Therefore, he should have his turn shooting and his share of the shells. They didn't see it that way. Another battle started over the shells and Herman lost again. They tied him up, sat him against the corner of the barn. With LeeRoy's help, they nailed his ear to the corner of the barn. That made sure he couldn't get loose and follow them. When Uncle Earl and Aunt Merle got home that day, there he was, secured to the barn, waiting for some one to pull the nail out and let him loose. He was probably the first male in Oklahoma to have a pierced ear.

There wasn't much those Rowland boys wouldn't do if they thought they could get away with it.

LeeRoy was probably the most ornery one in the Rowland clan, or even the whole community, for that matter. One Saturday, he took fifty cents from his money for picking cotton and bought a pint of Highlife at the drug store. I don't know what went into making Highlife, but I knew it brought animals to life and human beings, too. It looked just like water. Dad always had a bottle in the big chicken house. Occasionally he would pour a teaspoon full in the seed bins to kill the weevils and keep other bugs out. Once in a while James and I would take the bottle out when Daddy wasn't home and pour a little on the backs of animals. It would drive them crazy. They would run hog wild around the lot bucking, pitching and sometimes they would lie down and wallow in the dirt to stop the stinging or burning or whatever the Highlife did to them.

One day I took Dad's Highlife bottle and let a drop or two drip out on my hand, but it didn't affect me at all. It felt cool, and that was just about it. I mentioned it to James and he said it only affected animals that had hair. Well, I wasn't going to test it on my head, but I made other plans. The next day I coaxed my little sister, Betty Jo, into the big chicken house. I loosened the lid on the Highlife bottle and let about a teaspoon of it run out on her head. She had no reaction for a couple of seconds, then she let out a bellow that you could have heard clear to town. Mama heard her screaming and ran out the back of the house asking what happened. Betty Jo was bawling and running to meet her. They met right at the old iron wash pot. I yelled, "I poured Highlife on her head." Mama picked her up and shoved her head into the cold soapy water left in the pot from the last washing. When Betty Jo's head came out, she quit hollering and I headed for the pasture. That night Dad wore out a couple more mulberry switches on me.

Everybody in the community knew the effects of Highlife on animals. LeeRoy spent that Saturday night with us. As soon as the chores were finished the next morning, James, LeeRoy and I took off down the road early for Sunday school. LeeRoy had poured half of his Highlife into a half-pint whiskey bottle. It was easier to carry that way, and more importantly, easier to conceal.

We stopped at Grandpa Hunter's house and asked if we could ride on to Sunday school with them in their wagon. Mrs. Hunter said that would be fine but that we would have to wait awhile, because Mr. Hunter hadn't finished milking the cows. She invited us to come in the house and wait, or sit outside in the swing while she and the girls finished getting ready. We chose to sit outside in the swing on their porch. Mr. Hunter didn't go to Sunday school, so we would be riding with the women.

Their old dog had quit barking at us and had walked up close enough for us to pet. While James and I were petting the dog, LeeRoy was getting out his whiskey bottle. He loosened the cork and let a little Highlife dribble down to the skin across the dog's back. In about five seconds, the dog went into a wild-eyed fit. He was howling and circling the yard. Mr. Hunter had just come through the cow lot gate with big bucket of milk in each hand. On the third circle around the yard, the dog made a beeline for him. Mr. Hunter stopped and the dog nearly knocked him down. He spilled some of the milk and then the dog settled down. He said he wondered if the dog was going loco, had hydrophobia, or maybe it had worms.

When he got to the back door he said, "Why don't you boys come on into the house and have a more comfortable seat? The women will be ready before long. As soon as I strain this milk, you can help me harness the horses and hitch them up to the wagon."

We went into the house and the living room had only two chairs in it and one double bed. On the bed was a big old brown tomcat. LeeRoy naturally chose the bed for his seat, while James and I took the chairs. We could see Mr. Hunter through the kitchen door straining the milk through an old flour sack into a bigger bucket. When he finished, he set the big bucket of milk in the middle of the kitchen table and spread a dry flour sack over it to keep the flies out.

The women were in the bedrooms getting ready for church. Mr. Hunter turned his back to us and proceeded pour himself a cup of coffee out of an old gray enameled pot. LeeRoy had been petting the cat and this was the chance he had been waiting for. As Mr. Hunter was stirring sugar in his coffee, LeeRoy was loosening the cork on the whiskey bottle. The tomcat got his dose of Highlife and in five seconds was squalling and circling the room. Mrs. Hunter ran out of the bedroom in her petticoat to see what was going on. The cat jumped up on the kitchen cabinet and from it made giant leap to the table. Its feet didn't hit the tabletop, but they did hit in the middle of the flour sack over the big milk bucket. The flour sack gave way and the cat was baptized right there in that fresh milk. Now, both Mr. and Mrs. Hunter were wondering if all their animals had gone loco or had the worms. When the milk-drenched cat slowed down Mrs. Hunter let it out through the screen door.

We rode to the schoolhouse with them and attended our Bible classes. We kept the Highlife secret. Some parents would let their boys ride horses to Sunday school when the plowing was over. If they went home with anyone for dinner, they would share rides. It wasn't unusual for three or four horses to be walking side by side and two boys riding each of them on the way home from Sunday school. On that Sunday we had been invited to the home of the Frenches. They were new to our community that year. They had two boys about the same ages as James and me. They were Nazarenes and the only ones in our community. Dad said that they had a college in Bethany, Oklahoma, and that going there for a camp meeting of Nazarenes was about like going to heaven for them.

Mrs. French was recognized as one of the best Bible students in our community. She was a fine singer too. She could lead songs better than any of the men could. The only trouble the men wouldn't let her lead singing because women were forbidden to usurp authority over the men. However, when some man in authority was supposed to be leading the singing and couldn't get a song pitched right, he would ask Mrs. French to get it started and lead it from her seat. She apparently usurped her authority over the men only if she led the singing up front, but it was perfectly Scriptural if she was sitting down when she led it. The Bible seemed to be quite specific about where you were and whether you were sitting or standing when you did something religious, especially if you were a woman.

Their two boys were really straight-laced. We never heard them cuss or tell dirty stories. They were even stricter than the Baptists or the Holiness kids at not sinning like cussing, drinking, smoking and dancing. When Baptist strictness came up one time, dad said that the Baptists were too strict, especially on drinking and that he expected some of them to start drinking in public one of these days. Mom seemed to think that was really funny. I didn't get the joke.

The best Nazarenes claimed to be wholly sanctified in spirit, body and soul. Most other Christians were happy to just claim simple sanctification. Mrs. French said that when you had the second work of grace, as the Nazarenes taught, you would be above sinning. We had to admit they seemed to be about the most sinless family in the community. In discussing them one night, Daddy said that might be so, but you never knew what went on when the doors were shut and the curtains were pulled. He said he stopped by their house after dark one night and before he got to the door he could hear the two of them yelling at each other at the top of their voices. He said he decided not to knock on their door, because the way they were arguing, they didn't sound too holy, or wholly sanctified to him. But, he was willing to let God do the judging on it. He figured that he and mom had had a few loud fusses and they were still Christians, weren't they?

Anyway, the French boys were riding home from Sunday school that day, doubled up on one horse alongside three more horses with two boys each riding on their backs. LeeRoy was riding behind Roger, and he had him pull up beside the French boys' horse. Before long he was leaning over and resting with one elbow on their horse's rump. It took about two hundred yards for him to get his whiskey bottle out and loosen the cork unnoticed. He must have poured two tablespoons on their horse's rear end. In a few seconds it went into a wild running and bucking spree. The rest of us were yelling, "Ride 'em cowboy." By the time the horse made its fifth buck, both boys were thrown, and the rest of us got a big laugh. Roger ran on down the road to catch the

French boys' horse and bring it back, but they were afraid to get back on it. So they led it the rest of the way home.

LeeRoy's exploits with Highlife were well known. Everyone said he got his money's worth out of every pint of Highlife he ever bought.

On the Sunday afternoon of the rodeo, the three of us had a donkey on our hands, that was pretty tame and gentle. We tried to ride it, but without a bridle we couldn't get it to go where we wanted it to. We were about to abandon it when LeeRoy suggested that since it didn't have a brand or an ear tag, maybe it was abandoned by its owner here in the river bottom. "It could be ours for the taking," he argued. James and I didn't think that was a very good idea but LeeRoy was convincing. "But how will we get it home? We don't even have a rope to lead it with," James wondered. By this time we weren't wearing overalls much any more. The relief truck had come by the school and every boy in school got two pairs of black corduroy pants, so we used belts. "We can lead it with our two belts. We'll just buckle them together and they'll be long enough," was LeeRoy's solution.

James and I were still reluctant to take the donkey home. LeeRoy agreed that he would keep it at his house and tell his dad that it belonged to James. They would stick by a story that he had traded for it. "What can we claim we traded for it," James wanted to know. LeeRoy seemed to always have an answer. "We'll just say that we found two steel traps on the way to the rodeo beside the road in a bar ditch and traded them for the donkey."

In spite of that not being too plausible, it was an answer to the question. Our story to our dad would be that LeeRoy found two steel traps beside the road on the way to the rodeo and that he traded them to some guy at the rodeo for the donkey. But, the story they would tell uncle Earl, was that James had found the traps and that he had traded them for the donkey.

"What guy?" James wanted to know.

"Let's just make up a name. How about saying that there were two Marlin brothers at the rodeo who farmed in the tight land over by Texola. And, that they brought the donkey and it was a part of the rodeo because it really could buck. And the Marlin brothers were tired of feeding the otherwise useless beast and were glad to get two steel traps in exchange for it."

That was LeeRoy's solution to the problem of ownership. He could always think up lies for answers quicker than anyone else could think up the questions. In innocence, James responded, "But we don't know any Marlin brothers from Texola."

"That's the point, stupid. No one else does either. No one can prove they don't live there and that we didn't trade the two steel traps, that we didn't really find, for their donkey that really wasn't theirs."

That sounded pretty reasonable to James as he started taking off his belt. I thought that it would be both stealing and lying. They would be breaking two of the Ten Commandments — the ones against lying and stealing. I say, "They," because it was not my decision. I was just the little brother tagging along. I must admit I thought the idea would fly if we all stuck by the same story. I kind of liked the donkey myself. It would be a novelty to have around because hardly any family would keep an animal around that didn't somehow contribute to the family welfare. Dogs caught rabbits. Cats caught mice. Cows gave milk. Pigs furnished bacon, sausage and ham. Horses and mules pulled plows and wagons. What would this donkey contribute? I knew that would be among the first questions Uncle Earl or Daddy would ask.

They buckled our belts together and tied the end around the donkey's neck and we were off with the donkey switching its tail behind.

We were not halfway to Uncle Earl's before they decided to get the story straightened out a little more. Who would actually own this donkey? Whose donkey was it, James' or LeeRoy's? If James claimed it, LeeRoy couldn't claim ownership, and he couldn't give up that. Since we were getting to Uncle Earl's first, LeeRoy came up with a ready answer. We would tell Uncle Earl that the donkey belonged to James. He was the one who spotted the steel traps in the bar ditch. So, it was his steel traps that were traded. LeeRoy would get permission to spend Sunday night with us and we would take the donkey on to our house and tell my dad that the donkey belonged to LeeRoy. We would say that he had found two steel traps in the bar ditch and that he traded the traps for the donkey. That way all the bases would be covered and no one but us would ever know the difference.

When we got to Uncle Earl's house, everyone came out to inspect the donkey that James had traded his steel traps for. The first thing Uncle Earl said was, "Where did it come from?" LeeRoy and James told their story and explained how the ownership had passed from the Marlin brothers from Texola to James. Then Uncle Earl said, "Well I'm glad I don't have to feed the worthless beast." And he was glad to give LeeRoy permission to spend the night with us. Upon arrival at our house, Dad came out along with Mary and Ruth, and they inspected the donkey.

Dad's first question was, "Where did it come from?" James was eager to tell him.

"LeeRoy found two steel traps in the bar ditch beside the road on the way to the rodeo. And, he traded them to the Marlin boys from Texola for the donkey."

Dad said, "I don't know any Marlin boys who live in Texola." "They farm over in the tight land somewhere south of town," LeeRoy answered.

They hadn't counted on Dad knowing nearly everybody around Texola. But LeeRoy continued thinking up lies for answers faster than Dad was thinking up the questions. So, James and I were somewhat relieved.

Then Dad said, "Well I'm glad I don't have to feed the worthless beast." Dad and his older brother Earl thought exactly alike.

The next morning after the chores and breakfast, James and LeeRoy led their donkey, with a rope around its neck, off to school. They attracted every kid along the way, and by the time we arrived at school there were twenty kids in the donkey parade. The teachers weren't too happy to have a donkey at school, but they were willing to tolerate it. By this time the two cousins claimed to co-own the donkey. It was no longer James' donkey, as it was described at Uncle Earl's. Nor, was it LeeRoy's donkey as described at our house. The proud co-owners claimed the donkey and were willing to let anybody try to ride it after lunch. Later the teachers agreed to a Riverview School version of a rodeo if the donkey would buck. They figured it would be a diversion from the wrangling over strikes, balls and outs of the regular baseball games.

The older boys were offered the right to ride the donkey. At first there were only two who volunteered to try to ride it if it really bucked. A cershandle, made of the rope, was wrapped around the donkey's girth for the would-be cowboy to hang on to, and LeeRoy decided he would be the first one to ride his donkey. When he was on and had a good grip on the cershandle the donkey was turned loose. It just stood there. Everybody laughed. LeeRoy was embarrassed because he wasn't going to get to show off his rodeo skills. Roy Whitely reached over and tickled the donkey in the flanks and it gave a buck so high that LeeRoy came sailing off into the dirt. The donkey would buck after all. If it could throw LeeRoy with one big buck, what would it do if we had a cinch rope to go over its back and around both flanks? Three boys volunteered to allow their belts to be used as a flank cinch rope.

LeeRoy was still determined to ride the donkey first. The boys were scattered in a large circle around the donkey. Most of the girls were standing on the top of the storm cellar and watching. When LeeRoy was ready, with a good grip on the cershandle, the belts were cinched up tight around the donkey's flanks. It then went into a real bucking spree, and on the third buck, LeeRoy went sprawling on the ground and couldn't get up because his breath was knocked out. The two other boys tried riding it only to wind up on their butts in the dirt, too. They were Troy Mefford and Earl Weldon. Earl was born with an extra little thumb growing out of the joint of the thumb on his right hand. It was about half as big around as his regular thumb and about an inch long. He called it his lucky thumb. Dad said it might be lucky, but the real reason he had one was because Mr. and Mrs. Weldon were cousins. It wasn't a lucky thumb that day, because the donkey threw him off on the second buck. Troy didn't fare any better.

We had one boy in the eighth grade, Johnny Comstock, who was about two years older than the rest of his class. He said he could-and would-ride it. When he was ready for the flank cinch to be tightened, it was, and the donkey put on a great show of running and bucking. Johnny held on. The donkey was bucking and heading right for the barbed wire fence behind the boy's toilet. He bailed out just in time to not be cut to ribbons on the fence. He hit the ground on two feet and the donkey quit bucking. The kids all cheered for Johnny. Although he was never cheered for his speed in doing book-work, he received his honors that day. He was now the Bronc Riding Champion of the school. We gave him this honor, in spite of the fact that he had only ridden a donkey that was less than half the size of a real bronc. But, he had ridden it and bareback to boot.

Since Dad and Uncle Earl were unwilling to feed the worthless donkey, how were the two new owners going to maintain this prized possession?

LeeRoy came up with his ready answer that started with a question. "Why not just keep it here on the school grounds for the rest of the week? It could live off the grass next to the fence that is not worn into the ground by the feet of baseball players. There is plenty of grass to keep the donkey alive for a week. That will keep the grass down and we can have a rodeo every day at noon." Surely there would be boys other than Johnny who would try to ride it.

James and LeeRoy asked the teachers about it, assuring them that their dads would approve. The teachers did not object because the grass along the fence was already out of hand. So the front gate was closed each night and the donkey was to stay on the school ground for the week. James and LeeRoy would be pretty safe from prying questions that way, too. With the donkey at school they wouldn't have to think up answers to those questions.

The rodeo resumed after our lunches were eaten for the next three days. Johnny was still the only boy who could stay on the donkey.

On Thursday, right in the middle of the rodeo, and after a couple of boys had been thrown, a big open touring car drove up in front of the school. There were two men and two boys in it. I recognized one of the men and the two boys immediately. They were Mr. Hefner and his two boys from the Mayfield community, on the north side of the river. The other man was a stranger to us. All the younger kids ran up to the fender of the car to see who they were and what they wanted. The older boys kept holding rodeo.

The stranger stated, "I want to see the Rowland boys."

There were at least four of them in school.

"Which ones do you want?" someone asked.

"The ones who own that donkey," he answered.

By this time I was really glad that I had claimed no ownership in the donkey. But we called for James and LeeRoy to come over.

LeeRoy walked right up to the car as confident as a cat playing with a mouse. James was standing sort of at the back of the pack of kids with his head kind of hanging down. In fact, I could tell he was trying to hide behind our cowboy, Johnny.

"Yes Sir," LeeRoy boldly said. "What do you want?"

"I'd like to speak to the boys who own that donkey," he said.

"You're talking to one of them and the other is standing right back there behind that big feller named Johnny Comstock. What do you want to know?" said LeeRoy.

"Where did you get that donkey?" asked the man.

With a straight face LeeRoy answered, "We traded for it, Sir."

"What did you trade for it?"

"Two steel traps, Sir," said LeeRoy.

"Where did you get the steel traps?" he asked.

"We found them in a bar ditch beside the road between here and Red Bluff, Sir," said LeeRoy.

LeeRoy had never been this polite in his whole life. He never even addressed a teacher as "Ma'am." I think we were all impressed with his new-found manners. Sir this and Sir that rolled his tongue, along with lies, as smooth as honey.

The man then asked, "Who did you trade those two steel traps with to get the donkey?"

"The Marlin brothers. They said they lived in the tight land south of Texola," he lied through his teeth, but kept a straight face.

Both teachers then walked out to the meeting and stood by to see what was happening.

The stranger then reached in his shirt pocket and pulled out a shiny badge that identified him as a deputy sheriff.

He said, "I'm representing the sheriff of Beckham County, and I'm here to find out about the theft of a donkey that belongs to this gentleman here, Mr. Hefner. Everybody in this community knows that there is a new donkey here at the Riverview School, and Mr. Hefner says that donkey over there is his. He also says that he never traded or sold that donkey to anybody."

"But" LeeRoy interjected, and was still as cool as a cat, "James and I traded two steel traps we found in the bar ditch to the Marlin brothers for it." He turned to get James' corroboration on his story. James was nodding his head up and down, giving his support to the story while trying to exude confidence. But he wasn't saying a word and looked at the ground instead of at the deputy sheriff. He knew LeeRoy could lie better than he could. I did not nod, nor did I speak up. I was about to wet in my pants or something even worse. The truth was that James had already wet his pants when the man flashed his badge. He was wishing that he had gone down to the boys' toilet to hide, instead of following the crowd out to this touring car.

A ripple of fear also ran through the assembled students, and real fear ran through the two donkey thieves. This was something serious. You didn't have to be too smart to figure out that LeeRoy and James might have really stolen that donkey and that was the real reason to hide it on the school grounds.

The deputy sheriff and Mr. Hefner got out of the car and walked across the school ground to inspect the donkey. The deputy had pistol and handcuffs in scabbards on his belt. That certainly impressed us. I think it especially impressed James. The donkey looked no worse for the wear from the four days of bucking.

They waved for James and LeeRoy to come over, and they did. Some of the students were expecting them to be handcuffed and hauled off to the county jail in Sayre. They knew LeeRoy well enough to know that he was lying right through his teeth. They also knew that James had to back up the story, no matter how far fetched it was.

I was relieved that I had made no claim on the donkey and that no one could accuse me of breaking the law or the eighth and ninth commandments. Maybe I had already kind of broken the ninth commandment for not telling the truth when Daddy asked where we got the donkey in the first place. But I figured that you didn't actually lie unless you spoke it out of your own mouth. I knew that even if I was guilty a little bit, I could live with that amount of guilt without admitting anything — that is, unless it meant going to the reform school in Pauls Valley. Then I would even be willing to squeal on James and LeeRoy both if it meant that I wouldn't be arrested. Everybody would testify that I never claimed one hair of ownership in that donkey. If it meant that I could keep from going to Pauls Valley, I would testify that we didn't actually find the two steel traps and that LeeRoy made the whole story up. I would even testify that it was all LeeRoy's idea. After all, I didn't want my brother in the reform school. I especially didn't want the have to milk his cows for the next year and do his other chores while he was locked up.

When confronted by the deputy sheriff, and Mr. Hefner making an absolute claim that the donkey really belonged to him, LeeRoy said they could have it. This way the dispute over its ownership would be settled peacefully. He said that he reckoned that since they had found the steel traps in the bar ditch beside the road, that he and James weren't really out anything on it anyway.

They brought out a halter and a rope, tied the donkey to the back bumper of the car and headed off toward Mayfield with the donkey trotting behind.

Our noon rodeo was over.

That was a close one for those two Rowland boys. They nearly wound up in the Pauls Valley reformatory. In fact, they wondered later if the law might've put them straight in the prison at McAlester for being horse thieves. They never changed the story about the steel traps and the Marlin brothers, even though no one in the community now believed them. That night Daddy wore out two mulberry switches on James' rear end.

They should have listened to the song we sang often at Sunday school, "Yield not to temptation, for yielding is sin." James and LeeRoy weren't the only ones tempted to steal among the Rowland clans. I faced the temptation one summer day and Jimmy Trubbel wasn't even threatening me.

We were mowing hay, and the mower hit a Shinnery stob sticking out of the ground. Stobs are the remains of Shinnery roots after you cleared land. Every country boy had stobbed his toes on them dozens of times when running through the fields. Hitting that stob broke a couple of the sickle blades on the mower. The result was that it left streaks of uncut grass where the broken blades were. While Daddy had mowed, James and I stacked the cut hay into windrows with pitchforks. The hay would be picked up later when it was dry, and carried to our feedlot and stacked. There were at least ten acres that Dad had mowed when he hit the stob.

Dad decided that I would ride our mule, Kate, to town and buy two new blades for the sickle. We no longer had any credit at the hardware store. Therefore I would have to pay cash for the blades. Daddy didn't have any money, so it would be necessary for me to go the house, take a gallon of cream, and sell it at the creamery to get the money to buy the blades. I rode old Kate to the house and Mama gave me a gallon Jewel Lard bucket full of cream to take to town. While I went to town, Daddy and James would continue forking the newly cut hay into windrows.

It was nearly noon when I left. I asked Mama if I could get a hamburger with any money left over from buying the sickle blades. She said that it would be OK. Hamburgers were a nickel each, and so were soft drinks. The idea that there might be enough money left over to buy a hamburger, and maybe even a Delaware Punch, excited me.

When I got to the creamery, the owner tested our cream for butterfat content and then weighed it. He paid me sixty-eight cents for the cream. I then went to the hardware store and bought two sickle blades for twenty cents each. I was rich with twenty-eight cents in my pocket. I crossed the street to Aunt Carrie's Café and paid ten cents for a hamburger and a Delaware Punch.

After my meal I went into the Erick's Variety Store to see what I could buy for eighteen cents. I knew I would have to show up at home with some change. I decided that it would be eight cents.

I walked by the candy counter. My, it was tempting. I then sauntered around the store, rattling the coins in my hands to let the clerk know that I was a real customer. I stopped in front a counter that had the French harps on it. I picked one up and blew through it. The store had two kinds. One kind was a real harmonica and sold for thirty-five cents. The other was a cheap little contraption, made in Japan and sold for a mere dime.

I wanted the thirty-five cent harmonica but didn't have enough money. I could buy the dime one and have eight cents left over to buy candy if I wanted to spend all the cream money. While the store's lone clerk was waiting on someone else I decided I could have the best of the two worlds, the better harmonica, candy and still have eight cents left over. My arithmetic was pretty good, but my knowledge of competing forces around me was pretty bad. One of the forces would be my brother James.

I slipped the harmonica into my pocket and moved toward the candy counter. I bought two nickel Hershey bars and had eight cents left over. I high-tailed it out of the store with my candy, the stolen harmonica, the mower blades and eight cents. I climbed on old Kate and headed home.

When I finally got back to the hay field, I had already eaten one of the Hershey bars. I gave the other one to Dad and he divided it three ways between himself, James and me. I knew that I shouldn't take a share of the candy but to avoid suspicion I did. I was feeling real guilty for eating one all by myself. I also thought that if I gave that second candy bar to them, Daddy wouldn't be upset with me buying the cheap French harp. He might even think that I was very thoughtful. I was more than willing to share the French harp with the rest of he family. Daddy could actually play tunes on one.

Dad asked, "How much did the cream bring?"

"Sixty-eight cents," I answered.

"Then how did you buy the French harp?" James demanded.

"Mama said that I could spend some of the extra cream money for lunch. And, instead of buying my lunch I bought the French harp," was my reasonable reply.

"That's a bunch of bologna. You're a liar. Either you got more money for the cream or you stole the French harp. That harp costs thirty-five cents," he charged.

I hadn't counted on this outside force upsetting my perfectly laid out theft and the deception necessary to cover it up.

James looked at Daddy and claimed that he had picked up a French harp just like it last Saturday and it was priced at thirty-five cents. He claimed the dime ones were little cheap things made in Japan. He knew the difference and no amount of lying on my part was going to change the facts.

Daddy looked me right in the eye and asked, "Did you steal this French harp?" I was caught. There was no way out. No matter how much I coveted that better harp, my conscience would not let me lie further. I confessed that I stole the harmonica.

Immediately James asked, "Then what happened to the rest of the money?" I was caught again. Dad looked at me with inquiring eyes. I said that I spent forty cents on the mower blades, ten cents for lunch, ten cents on two bars of candy and had eight cents left over. I confessed to eating one of the bars on the way home. My arithmetic was not fast enough to fool either one. It was too late to change my story on how much the cream brought to cover my tracks about the French

My maternal grandparents, Mr. and Mrs. Robert M. Houston of Idabel, Oklahoma. They came to Oklahoma from Kentucky in 1909. I lived with them for one semester during my freshman year in high school. We rode that buggy to town and church.

Mr. and Mrs. Will Rowland, my paternal grandparents. They came to Oklahoma from Missouri in 1908, the year after statehood.

My parents, Roger Sherman Rowland and Elizabeth Ann Houston, on the day he proposed to her in November, 1920 at Smithville, Oklahoma, where she taught school.

Our family of six in front of the mulberry tree and the big chicken house in 1929.

Our family grew to eight and each year there
seemed to be fewer switches on the lower limbs
of the old mulberry tree. Ruth took this picture.

A big gathering of the Rowland, Dobson, Hunter and Powers clans for a
Sunday chicken dinner at our house.

Riverview kids in their Sunday best. Mary and Ruth with their fur collars. James was wearing the cap in the back and I'm on the right. Goober was between us wearing the aviator's cap.

Empty store and bank buildings line Erick's Main Street now just as they did at the end of the Great Depression.

Getting paid for climbing Erick's water tower was a temptation Goober Powers could not resist. It was the high-light of the week in Erick.

Fourth grade boys. Front row: Bob Rowland, Harrel Ray Whitely and Taylor Comstock. Back row: Goober Powers, Junior Tigner, and Troy Wildmon.

The migration of "Okies" to California during the Great Depression left Riverview School with just enough pupils for one teacher. Pictured are grades one through eight in 1935. The school closed in about 1938.

harp and the candy bar.

"That comes to sixty-eight cents," James figured.

Dad said, "I don't know what's going to happen to you boys. One steals a donkey, then lies about it. The other one steals a French harp and lies about it, as well as covering up eating at Aunt Carrie's and buying candy. If you boys don't straighten up you are going to wind up in Pauls Valley or McAlester. Bob, next Saturday you are going to go into the Variety Store and confess this theft to the manager. Then you are going to have pay for it from your first cotton-picking money this fall." And that I did. The threat of Pauls Valley alone hung pretty heavy over our heads when it was mentioned, and when the McAlester State Penitentiary was mentioned that was a lot heavier. We did not want to go to either place and were determined to behave better.

James had already pretty well overcome his conscience wounds for stealing the donkey and I was just beginning to face my guilt over the use of, and the lying about the use of, the money from the cream.

We didn't wind up with any scars from these incidents, nor did either of us go to jail. But, there would be other events that left scars on my head that joined the one put there by TooWoo Tompson' lunch bucket.

CHAPTER 8

SLINGSHOTS, IRON SLUGS AND SCARS

Every respectable boy in any Oklahoma country elementary school had a slingshot and knew how to use it. Most country boys cut a forked limb off of a tree about an inch in diameter and six inches long. They peeled its bark off and tied rubber bands from old inner tubes on the end of each fork. On the other end of the rubber bands they tied a pouch of some kind. Most of these boys carried their slingshots everywhere they went, except to school. School was off limits for slingshots because someone might get an eye put out.

The slingshots were used for lots of purposes, but mostly for target shooting. They came in handy for killing snakes and ground squirrels. They weren't powerful enough to kill a rabbit unless you were up really close and the rabbit was sitting still. You could also shoot a bird if it was sitting still on its nest or a tree limb. Birds were our primary targets when we went hunting with slingshots.

On nearly every farm there were one or two old Model-T Fords, Chevrolets, Hudsons, Graham-Paiges or similar cars around that were beyond repair. Some had gone through two or three engines. These useless engines were dumped, along with other trash, somewhere on all farms. Their blocks were made of cast iron and we used a hammer to break them up and into small pieces. These iron slug pieces made great ammunition for our slingshots. Any boy worth his salt could find a few small rocks to shoot with. Comparing iron slugs to rocks was the equivalent a gangster carrying a Tommy Gun and comparing it to a policeman carrying a single shot 22. A boy with a slingshot and a few iron slugs was the natural extension of the primordial instincts that led cavemen to go out and capture or kill game for his family.

Jenks Dobson was considered one of the best shots in the Riverview Community. He could hit the bull's-eye in the center of a target painted on the back of the barn nearly every time. Boys with slingshots and iron slugs, were threats to every bird in the county.

On one trip between the Dobson house and ours, James and Jenks were carrying brand new slingshots made from pine boards, and not from tree branches. Mr. Dobson had let them use his coping saw to cut them out handles from his clear one-by-four pine boards. Their handles were beauties. No one else had a pine board sling shot in the whole community. The rubber bands were attached to the forks on the handle and to an old shoe tongue pouch on the other end. The rubber bands came off of a genuine Goodyear inner tube. Mr. Dobson was a carpenter and a cabinetmaker. He was the only person who had clear one-by-four boards in the whole community. These slingshots were special.

Jenks set out to prove to James and me that he could hit any bird in a nest or on a tree limb. Moreover, it was known by everyone in the community that he could actually shoot a bird's head clean off. This was due to his great accuracy and the sharp edges of his iron slugs. The first bird we came upon was a dove on a nest about twenty feet up in a big cottonwood tree.

The dove didn't move but it did keep its eye on us. Jenks moved around until he was in the best position to hit it. He drew his pouch back loaded with an iron slug and let it fly. The dove tumbled out of its nest and before you could say "Jack Robinson" Jenks rushed into the bushes where the dove fell and brought it out with its head knocked completely off. "Wow!" I exclaimed. James was also duly impressed. Jenks had a look of great satisfaction on his face as well. That was one headless dove in the pocket for supper, and the hunt was on for more.

We crossed the fence and into the pasture of Mr. Norman Williams. There were a number of Shinnery patches scattered through all pastures that were havens for rabbits and all kind of birds. The Shinnery bushes didn't grow but about fifteen feet high and were in patches from thirty to fifty feet in diameter. There they grew thick and fast. We got all our firewood and fence posts from these patches.

Sure enough there were a number of nests in the first patch we went to. On one nest sat another dove. Jenks lined up his slingshot and let an iron slug fly. That dove tumbled out of its nest into the bushes and grass below it. Jenks again rushed in and brought out another dove with its head shot clean off. After a few additional wows by James and me, the rest of the birds in that patch were scared off. So it was on to another Shinnery patch with two doves in hand.

Jenks again found a bird on its nest, but this time it was a mocking bird. Our caveman instincts did not differentiate between birds you could eat and any other kind. Although we never ate them, mocking birds were just as fair game as doves were. Again Jenks was lining up his slingshot at the mocking bird that was not more than ten feet away. He let another iron slug fly. The bird tumbled to the ground and all three of us ran to get it. Its head was intact. James became suspicious of the hotshot bird killer. "If he was so good why didn't he knock its head off?" We wondered. On the next kill, James ran over to the kill and caught Jenks yanking the bird's head off and dropping it to the ground to make it look like he had actually shot it off. We accused him of doing the same thing to the rest of the birds.

He could no longer make the claim of being accurate enough to shoot birds' heads off every time. From that day on, he was somewhat discredited at the Riverview school, even though he was still about the best slingshot shooter in the community.

I didn't always carry my slingshot with me, but James always did. He carried iron slugs around so long that they finally cut holes in his pockets and through the leg of his pants as well. It seemed that mom patched one of his pockets nearly every other week.

One summer day when James and I were plowing the crops with two wheeled cultivators, we had another of those unforgettable experiences. Dad was away on a WPA project with the wagon and one team of horses. James and I were left to do the farming with the other two teams.

Each morning the cows were fed, milked, watered and put out to pasture. Then the horses were fed. If there wasn't enough wind to turn the windmill, the barrel full of water had to be pumped by hand. The hogs were slopped after we had eaten breakfast. We would then harness our teams, go the fields, and plow until noon. At noon we brought the teams in, fed and watered them. We then ate dinner and took a nap while the horses rested down by the barn in the horse lot. We always removed their harnesses during these noon breaks so the horses could rest better.

Since Daddy was away on the WPA road job, James felt like he was in charge. Mom had enough to do in keeping herself and the older girls busy washing clothes, ironing, working the garden, canning and picking Lambs Quarter to make greens for the table. The girls would scour the roads and fence-rows to get enough Lambs Quarter greens to supplement our red beans and cornbread. When they couldn't gather enough Lambs Quarter, they gathered another weed, called Careless Weed, to make up the difference. The women also had our four-year-old Jo and baby brother Rick to care for. She was so busy with household tasks that she left the farming up to James and me. But James really believed that the supervision of the farming was left up to him alone. I resented his bossing, and regularly tested his authority.

One day at noon, I was taking my nap on the Bermuda grass next to the windmill and in its shade. James always took his noon nap on a mattress we slept on during the summer months under a big cottonwood tree in our back yard. He woke up and yelled to me that it was time to "Grab a root and growl" because that was always what Daddy shouted after dinner and our noon naps. I wasn't quite ready to grab a root, but I was willing to growl. I growled that my nap wasn't quite up. He stopped by the windmill and took a drink with an old gourd dipper hanging on the fresh water keg. He said, "Come on." He then went to the barn to harness his horses. I drove my plow with a team of mules, Kit and Kate. But I wasn't ready to harness them yet.

When he finished harnessing his horses, he yelled out another order, "Get up here and harness these mules. We've got to get to the field!" I was lying on my stomach with my straw hat over the back of my head, giving me a little extra shade from the noon day sun. James had his horses harnessed and was waiting for me to obey his orders. When I refused to budge, he threatened to go the house to tell Mom. But, doing that would be an admission that he wasn't really the boss. Mom wasn't through with her nap, either. He knew that she might get just about as testy with him for awakening her, as much maybe as she would be with my delay in harnessing my mules.

James then resorted to a threat that he seldom made because it was a definite "No-No" anyway, any time, and anywhere. No one, but the school idiot would shoot at someone else with a sling shot, because you could put an eye out.

He yelled, "If you don't get up here this very minute, I'm going to shoot you with my slingshot." "And," he added, "with an iron slug, to boot."

I wasn't afraid of the threat, but I did sneak a peek out from under the brim of my straw hat in his direction. I noticed that he was standing beside Old Tony with his sling shot in his hand. Even if he did shoot an iron slug my way, he wouldn't shoot it directly at me. Even if he shot at me he probably wouldn't hit me from that distance. I figured that he might shoot it close enough to try to scare me but he would never shoot at me. So, I just closed my eyes, turned my face away and ignored him.

He had decided to shoot a warning shot and let me know that he meant business. But I still knew he wouldn't try to hit me. Mom would give him a whipping and when dad got home Friday night he would be in for a worse one. This was another one of dad's rules that he never broke either. "If Mom had to whip us when he was gone, we'd get another whipping when he got home."

James did load the slingshot with an iron slug and shot an arching shot my way with no intention of hitting me. Or, so he said. It had a high trajectory and arched, unknown to me, not only in my direction but it was coming down right at my head.

By this time my eyes were good and shut. "Wham" something hit my head. It hit it hard. It was an iron slug and it cut right through my straw hat leaving a gash in my scalp, right beside TooWoo's scar. I reached back to inspect the damage and my hand revealed that my head was bleeding. I yelled for Mama about as loud as I could. I sounded like Joe Morris had that day I barbered and I was bleeding just about as bad, too. I started for the house in a dead run, holding the back of my head with my right hand.

James dove under the horse lot gate, zipped past the mulberry tree, and intercepted me before I got three-fourths of the way to the house. He tackled me and wouldn't let me up. I was wishing that I had another big brother that would interfere like David Morris had done that day for Joe. James was holding me down and begging me not to tell Mama. He then began making promises.

"I'll harness your horses all next week at noon if you don't tell," he offered.

"No!" I replied.

"I'll harness them every morning and at noon for the week, if you won't tell on me," he pleaded. He was pleading and was also crying nearly as loud as I was.

That was a pretty fair offer and my head wasn't hurting that much any way. It was just that all that blood from the head wound that was so scary. He didn't offer me his slingshot for my silence. But, I would bargain for it later. He did take me down to the windmill and gently washed the blood out of my hair. He harnessed my mules and we went to the field. For the next week, my free time after breakfast and dinner were extended while James harnessed both teams.

It took us about another week to finish plowing the cotton. My scalp was just about healed. Our maize field was the next to be plowed. When two cultivators were used for plowing the same field, one would start on the first row and the other would skip about twenty rows to start his plowing. This way we were always about fifty feet apart, and the dust from one person's plow would not blow into the face of the other. If the wind was just right, you could breathe enough dust to choke a mule from your own plow. That was bad enough by itself.

Every morning and afternoon we would take a half-gallon Mason jar of water to the field with us. It was covered with a tow sack that we dipped in the horse tank to get it wet before we left for the field. The wet tow sack would help keep the water in the jar cool a little longer. One of us would hang the jar of water on a plow handle and then we would stop periodically to take a drink. We usually stopped three times in an afternoon to drink, and at the third stop, we would finish the water. With the tow sack around the jar, you never knew how much water was left in it without looking in or giving it a good shake.

One afternoon, it was extra hot and James was carrying our jar of water on his plow handle. That day at each stop, as always, we not only had our water, but we also stopped long enough to let our teams take a short rest. With nothing to do but sit on an iron plow seat, while plowing row after row of various crops, we had plenty of time to think up riddles, jokes, word games and tall tails. These we shared at the rest and water stops to break the monotony of plowing. On the last water and rest stop one day, James had thought up a big yarn and spent extra time spieling it. I took the jar from the plow handle and twisted the cap off. It was about a third full and I was really hot and thirsty. We had an understanding that the one who drank first would leave an equal amount in the jar for the other. James talked on. I drank on.

I listened to his yarn while drinking more than my share of the remaining water. I reasoned that since I had drunk more than half of the water already, I wouldn't be much worse off if I drank more. So, I kept sipping and James kept telling me his big yarn. I noticed that there were only a couple of swallows of water left in the jar so I quit drinking and tightened the lid down as tight as I could. James finished his yarn with satisfaction on his face. I hung the jar back on his plow handle and said, "Well, I better get to plowing."

I started walking briskly toward my plow. After about five steps I broke into a dead run. James was immediately suspicious. He shook the jar and realized from the sound of the water that I had just about finished it. He reached for the slingshot in his hip pocket with his right hand and then for an iron slug in the front one with the left one. He pulled that loaded pouch back and let the iron slug fly. He was about as good a shot as Jenks. And this shot at me, a moving target, proved it.

The slug hit me right in the back of the head, cut through my straw hat and cut another hole in my scalp on the other side of my reminder of TooWoo's lunch bucket. I tumbled to the ground like I was half killed and by this time he was running toward me. I grabbed my hat with one hand and my new wound with the other one. I was heading for home and was really going to tell Mama this time. Again he tackled me. Not only was I bleeding, but he had me down in the dirt and I was getting it into my wound. He was begging me to stay in the field and tell no one. He said that I didn't have to plow any more that day. He would let me go over and rest in the shade of the Shinnery trees until quitting time.

"How generous," I sobbed between howls.

"I'll harness your mules morning and noon for a whole week again if you won't tell Mama."

"That'll be the day," I responded to his offer.

That was the day that I came to understand that knowledge is power.

"Please? Please, don't tell her, because she'll tell Daddy, and you know what that means." He was pleading almost in tears again. I had the upper hand and I was determined to bargain with it.

He then began to really cry. I wasn't sure the tears were out of the fear of what both Mama and Daddy would do or over my new wound and my pain and suffering. I hoped he had as much sympathy for me as he had fear for our parents.

"I won't tell, if you'll throw in your slingshot and iron slugs in the deal," I offered.

"It's done," was his reply.

He handed me his pretty pine board slingshot and the remaining iron slugs in his pocket. By now the blood was no longer running but it was mixed with dirt and was drying in my hair. James went for the remaining water and used it to wash my hair out the best he could, lest Mama discover my wound and his dastardly deed. He harnessed my mules for another week. I carried my pine board slingshot for a long time knowing that only Jenks Dobson, Riverview community's best shot, owned one like it.

Later in the summer, we moved our mattress inside, due the arrival of mosquitoes. Sleeping in the bed and on bedsprings was better anyway. But it was cool only when the windows and doors were all open and breeze was blowing through the house.

We had Jerry-rigged a shower down at the windmill with an old leaky milk bucket. We punched a few extra holes in its bottom and hung it on a cross brace on the windmill tower. One of us would dip water out of the water keg and climb up on the windmill tower and pour water into the leaky bucket. The other one would stand naked under the improvised shower and wash the dirt off. We would enter the back door next to our bedroom and sleep naked throughout the summer.

On one Friday night, Dad had come in from the WPA work camp, had bite to eat and went down to the windmill to pour water while James showered. The rest of us were playing hide and seek. Dad stayed down at the barn to check on the cows, pigs and feed supplies. James came to the house and went to bed.

I thought Dad had also brought home a pint of rot gut whiskey he occasionally bought from the town's bootlegger. Not only was Mom a Woman's Christian Temperance Union type, she was also a member. She praised President Franklin D. Roosevelt for all his alphabet programs designed to help the poor, but she would refuse to vote for him again because she held him personally responsible for the repeal of prohibition. She claimed that neither a liquor bottle, nor a cigarette butt had ever touched her lips.

Oklahoma was a dry state. At least it was legally. Yet, there wasn't a town that did not have at least one bootlegger who could furnish anyone with a bottle of moonshine if they had the money. There were a lot of farms all over the state that had a keg of home brew working under the haystack, or secreted away in some Shinnery patch. There were news stories of moonshine whiskey stills that were found and destroyed by the Revenue agents.

I think Dad was down at the barn on that night, taking a nip or two while enjoying this evening being home and away from the camp.

James had crawled into bed naked as a Jay-bird. He wanted to go to sleep. But Mary, Ruth and I were making so much noise he couldn't. He yelled at us to quiet down, but we didn't. Finally, Mom told us to quit running through the house and to go outside if we wanted to make noise. Mary and Ruth didn't want to go outside and play. They found something better and quieter to do inside. They began playing Chinese checkers. I also found something to do.

I walked through the open bedroom door quietly, reached through the bedstead and tickled James' feet. Then I scampered off as fast as I could. In a few minutes, I sneaked back in and tickled them again. That was enough for him.

"Bob Rowland" he yelled, "if you wake me up again I'll knock you in the head with the clothes brush." We had had that clothes brush as long as I could remember. It was made of oak and bristles. It was about two inches wide and eight inches long. The oak was about an inch thick. I figured that even if he threw it and hit me, I had a fifty-fifty chance of it hitting me on the bristle side that would be softer.

But I didn't really believe he meant it. I was also confident that if I sneaked in quietly and lower than the foot end of the bed, I could tickle his feet and get away before he could wake up, rise up, grab and throw the brush. Moreover, I would be a moving target. However, it would become clear to me shortly that I hadn't learned my lesson about his ability to hit moving targets.

I waited for a long time, giving him plenty of time to get to sleep before I sneaked back in. I didn't realize that he was not even trying to go to sleep. Instead, he was lying in wait for me.

I slipped in, and as I reached for his feet, he raised up in the bed. He threw the clothes brush as hard as he could, claiming afterwards that he was only trying to scare me. And, maybe he was. But he didn't scare me. He hit me right on the hairline just above my right eye. It knocked me down and I came up bleeding again. In fact, it was about the worst bleeding of any of my battle wounds to date, because the blood was running down my face. I let out a scream so loud that you could hear it all the way to the barn.

Dad heard me scream. He left doing whatever he was doing down at the barn and ran to the house. He already had his belt off and was ready to whip my butt for startling him. I was doubled up on the floor wailing away. He grabbed my arm with his left hand and drew back the belt with his right one. Just as he started to swing he saw the blood on my head and face.

"What happened?" he demanded.

"James hit me in the head with the clothes brush," I wailed.

James was standing naked in the middle of the bed and had no time to make his defense. Before he could say, "Bob started it," Dad yanked him off the bed and wore him out. I didn't even get a lick because Dad must have figured that the hole in my scalp was punishment enough. I started parting my hair from then on right where that hair brush left its scar.

Rot gut liquor and home brew would raise their heads many times in our community in the days ahead. In fact, I was to try out some spirits myself very shortly.

CHAPTER 9
WHEN ONE LITTLE NIP ISN'T ENOUGH

By the fourth grade, I had only seen one person drunk in my life. There were lots of stories running around about the town drunks, moonshiners, bootleggers and stills. I had only tasted beer a couple of times in my life. My dad had some bottles of beer hidden in the barn under the feed maize. He had a few bottles hidden in the cotton seed bin, too. Mom knew about it, but she didn't approve and didn't mind saying so. Dad kept a count on how many bottles he had stored away and drank, so there was little chance that James and I would ever swipe a bottle and try some.

Uncle Earl didn't mind letting people know that he made home brew. Aunt Merle didn't mind tipping a bottle or two of it when it was brewed. Our oldest cousins had enjoyed a few bottles and didn't mind bragging about it. One night I stayed all night at Uncle Earl's. After supper, we went down to the barn and Uncle Earl brought out four long necked bottles of beer he had cooling in the horse tank. He opened them and handed two to the boys and took two to the house for himself and Aunt Merle to drink.

Darrel and Roger were sharing a bottle, as were Herman and LeeRoy. They were passing the bottles back and forth as I stood by, hoping I would be given a sip. Finally Darrel asked me if I wanted some. Yes, of course I did! This was forbidden fruit and forbidden fruit makes the fruit taste twice as good. He offered me the bottle when there was only one little swig left in the bottom. I drank it, and then Herman offered me the last little bit left in the other bottle.

I felt important and I felt guilty. My mom would have condemned Uncle Earl for both having beer and drinking it. She really would have been on him, like a chicken on a grasshopper, if she had any idea that he or his boys had let me drink some beer.

For the next few days, I had some bragging rights about drinking beer, even if it was just a couple of swallows.

Oklahoma was still dry, and the preachers of every sect or denomination preached against liquor traffic and John Barleycorn. There was only one Catholic family that anybody knew of in the whole area. The Catholics were condemned regularly by all the Protestants, not only on the grounds that they had a Pope, but because they used real wine in their communion. In fact, I would forever associate the 666 mark of the beast in the book of Revelation with the Catholic Church. Nearly every preacher, regardless of denominational stripe, included one sermon in revivals on liquor and one on the "Mark of the Beast." It was always interpreted the same way. Hadn't the country made it clear in the election of 1928 that they wouldn't put a papist in the presidency like Al Smith? Anybody who knew anything about the Catholic religion, knew that a Catholic president would be loyal to the Pope in Rome, and not to the United States Constitution! If he had become president, we would all be walking around with "666," the "Mark of the Beast," on our foreheads. Beside all this, everybody also knew that Al Smith opposed prohibition and that was just about as bad. Everything we learned about the Catholics was learned through preachers who denounced them. They were never even given a chance to defend themselves. We never heard them preach what they believed. If it came to a vote in the Riverview community, Albert and Geraldine Jackson, who promoted no church, would have been the only citizens to vote for letting them use the schoolhouse for mass.

One Sunday there was a big discussion in Sunday school about prohibition. Publicly, nearly everyone who spoke up was for it, even if they had a keg or two of home brew working in their barns or Shinnery patches. Uncle Earl was about the only one who defended drinking in moderation, even though he seldom drank in moderation. He accused nearly everybody — Baptists, Methodists, Holiness members and Church of Christ members — of being hypocrites. He claimed that Jesus came eating and drinking, and that's why he was called a glutton and winebibber. He said that Jesus turned water into wine in Cana at the wedding feast, and it turned out to be the best wine at the feast. Pearl Whitely spoke up and said that she knew he did, but she would think a lot more of him if he hadn't. Uncle Earl then replied that Paul had told Timothy to drink wine for his stomach's sake. He knew all the Bible passages that promoted drinking, even if he couldn't quote hardly any other passages. Mrs. Whitely then corrected him on his quote from Paul. She said, "Paul told Timothy to drink a 'little' wine, not just any amount of wine."

So the battle went on between the dry forces and the wet ones all over the county and the state.

One day, Dad came in from fixing fences and told Mama that he and the boys, meaning James and I, were going rabbit hunting. He said he had seen quite a few rabbits in the forty acres of pasture on Grandpa Rowland's place. This pasture was about half grass and the rest was comprised of bushes, Shinnery patches, rotting logs and piles of brush cut off the trees we had cut down for firewood.

We took the dogs and went hunting. When we got to the forty acres of pasture Dad didn't seem too interested in hunting. We went right to the biggest Shinnery patch in the pasture. Dad entered the patch and called for us to come in. When we found him, he was smiling and sitting beside a twenty-five gallon keg of beer. It had a big cork in the bunghole. There was no way that I could see that he was going to be able to do what that smile on his face said he was going to do. There was no way, even with the help of us boys, was he going to drink out of that big keg through its bung hole. But we quickly learned how it was done by the pros. He went over to a big clump of Johnson grass and brought back a few stalks. He stripped the blades off, cut the joints off the ends of the grass stems with his pocketknife, leaving perfectly hollow straws for drinking. We took our turns sucking up the beer. He didn't let us drink much, but he had his fill.

James and I figured that he had watched one of our neighbors cross that pasture with his wagon, or had seen wagon tracks going toward the Shinnery patch. And, he suspected what he was up to. If a Revenuer searched that pasture, the beer would have belonged to Dad and he would have been held culpable, not our neighbor. But on this day, Dad had the best of both worlds. He doubted that anyone was likely to go to jail for having one twenty-five gallon keg of beer, and he had all the beer he wanted, when he wanted it, without the trouble and expense of making it.

The very next Sunday, we went home from Sunday school with the Dobsons. In the middle of the afternoon, James and I volunteered to go home and do all the chores. As we usually did on Sunday nights in the summer, nearly everybody in the community would meet at the schoolhouse for a community gospel singing. Dad said it was OK, and Jenks came along to help out.

We had a motive in volunteering that was different from milking the cows, feeding horses, chopping the wood, pumping water and slopping the hogs. We had visions of sucking all the beer we would ever want through Johnson grass straws.

As soon as we got out of sight of the Dobson house, we cut across the fields and the pasture, directly to the keg of beer. Jenks was in on our plan and we were happy to introduce him to beer. We surrounded the keg and were ready to take turns with our Johnson grass straws.

I couldn't drink nearly as much as James could. This was going to be the first time Jenks had ever tasted beer. His dad was a teetotaler and a preacher for the Christian Advent Church. They didn't drink any kind of booze, in secret or otherwise. When it was Jenks' turn to use his straw, he bent over the keg and took a sniff at the bunghole. He drew back and told us it smelled like horse piss. Jenks' comparison was probably right. But, you didn't get many chances to partake of such an abundance of forbidden fruit in the Riverview community. So you had better take it now. James and I had taken about three turns at the bunghole before Jenks decided to violate his dad's rule and his own conscience. He bent over and took a big draw on the straw. He quickly spit the beer out and told us that the stuff tasted like horse piss, too. He wanted no more of it. I asked him how he knew it tasted like horse piss. He said that he just knew.

When James and I had imbibed as much as we wanted, we pushed the cork stopper back into the bunghole.

James asked, "Why don't we just steal this beer?"

The owner didn't have a right to put it on our property anyway, he argued. But how would we transport it to some safe place where we could come and drink our fill anytime we wanted to? We decided that we would just carry it to another Shinnery patch and cover it with grass, leaves and brush. We may have been a little wobbly and not thinking too clearly on how to make this theft successful, due to the beer we had consumed. We didn't get ten feet trying to carry it. The closest Shinnery patch was at least a hundred yards away. So, we decided to roll it there. About half way the cork got knocked out and we spilled at least a gallon of the beer.

When we got the keg to the destination, we placed it in the middle of the patch and covered it very well with brush, leaves and grass. We knew that no one could ever find it. We then hurried about doing the chores and went to the evening singing at the schoolhouse. We bragged to the other boys about our stash of beer and how good it was. We were the envy of nearly every boy in the community. Older boys begged us to tell them where the keg was hidden, but we refused to divulge its location.

The very next night, as soon as we got home from school we went directly to the pasture to get the cows. We raced the last fifty yards to the Shinnery patch. To our surprise, someone had found the beer and had taken it away. There were wagon tracks right up the patch where the keg had been loaded. No doubt it was loaded by its true owner.

Our neighbor didn't have to be a genius to figure out how and where his beer had disappeared to. There was a clearly marked trail of a keg of beer being rolled from one patch to another, along with the tracks of the three boys who had rolled it there.

A couple of weeks later, news spread like wildfire that the revenuers had arrested Jim Deathridge and his brother for running a still. Apparently the revenuers had sat across Red River with field glasses for weeks. After they caught them red-handed and arrested them, they had blown the still to smithereens with dynamite.

Like most other crooks, Ben and brother weren't too smart. Buying fifty-gallon wooden barrels, hundred-pound sacks of sugar and barley from merchants in town would tip anybody off. Everybody knew that they weren't feeding cattle and hogs with it. So they had to be making moonshine. It didn't take long for some prohibitionist to become an informer.

On the Sunday afternoon following the blowing up of the still, James, Goober and I went to look at the destruction. We found barrel rims and staves, tubing, stoves and other paraphernalia for making whisky blown all to pieces. There was a barrel in the corner of the still that was intact and nearly full of beer. It was covered with dead moths and other insects. But one sniff told us that it was still the real thing. We skimmed the bugs off the top and started using Johnson grass straws. It took only one sip or two for us to agree with Jenks Dobson. This stuff really did taste like horse piss. At least it tasted like horse piss smelled.

It was in early summer that I decided to make a little moonshine myself. Well it wasn't going to be real moonshine — it was going to be wine. Along the river banks there were lots of wild grapes growing. When we were caught up with the plowing and chopping cotton, we often went down at the river to pick wild grapes and wild plums. Mom would make grape syrup out of half the grape juice. She would can the rest to drink later on. The wild plums were turned into plum jelly. In the storm cellar, there was a whole shelf of canned jars of grape juice in half-gallon Mason jars and a shelf of pint Mason jars full of plum jelly. That was enough to last us all winter.

One Saturday when the whole family was in town except Mama, the two youngest kids and me, I told her that I was going down to the river and pick myself some grapes to make my own grape juice. James had learned something about making wine from our cousins. He told me that after you squeezed the juice out of the grapes, all you had to do was to put a little yeast and sugar in it, for it to ferment. My purpose in going to the river was to pick enough grapes to make a half-gallon of wine. But, I knew Mom wouldn't give me any yeast or sugar to make it with. I would have to find another source. I picked wild grapes all afternoon to get a half of a tow sack full.

When I got home I squeezed the grapes and the juice nearly filled a half-gallon jar. When I showed Mama the jar of juice, all she said was that that was nice. I asked her for some sugar to sweeten it, as if I thought she might relent and give me some.

She said, "No, No, young man! And, I know how much sugar is in the sack too, so don't try anything funny." Obviously she was on to me.

I had a half-gallon of grape juice ready to start working into real wine and I couldn't even get a cup of sugar to get it started.

While sitting at the table looking at my grape juice, I realized that the grape syrup in the pitcher on the table was half sugar. At my first chance I poured half of the syrup out of the pitcher into my jar of juice. Thus, I had not actually disobeyed Mama. I did not actually steal any sugar. I had merely used grape syrup. She was keeping track of the sugar, but she wasn't watching the syrup. Later I slipped a few granules of yeast out in my pocket and added them to my concoction.

I knew I couldn't keep my wine around the barn because James would learn about it, find it and help himself to it. I took it down to a creek that ran through our pasture and hid it in behind some grapevines. I covered it with grass and no one would find it without a lot of effort. The grapevines had grown down a steep bank on the backside of the drinking pond we had created for our livestock.

Every night, on the way to river bottom to round up the cows, I would walk by my hiding place, but I kept about fifteen feet from it so I wouldn't leave a trail. After a couple of weeks, I took a sip of it. It was working, and left a kind of stinging sensation on my tongue. Wow! This was going to be great! I bragged about it to the boys at Sunday school. Goober thought I was really doing something big. I agreed to let him share a little when it was completely fermented. I continued to test it every five or six days. It was getting better each time. Just as summer was ending, the wine was ready, and I was ready.

I told Goober that he should watch our wagon when it went to town the next Saturday. If everybody in the family but me was in it, then he would know that I had permission to stay home by myself.

That would be his signal to stay home, too. He was then to get permission from his mom to come over to our house instead of going to town with his dad and brothers.

His mom had tuberculosis and was bedfast. She never went to town, to Sunday services or even school graduations. When I visited their house, I was a little afraid of going in the house and catching TB. But I would risk going into the kitchen and speaking to her through the door. She was very nice and was always propped up in bed. After Goober's dad and brothers left for town, she gave him permission to go to our place to go hunting with me.

We weren't interested in hunting, at least on that afternoon. As soon as he arrived, we high-tailed it to the creek. The grapevines, behind which my wine was hidden, were behind that small pond, formed by a small dam we had built across the creek. The pond was about a foot deep, ten feet wide and twenty feet long. I rushed around the pond, pulled the vines back and removed the dead dry grass hiding my wine.

I brought out a half-gallon jar full of fresh wine. Wow! I screwed the lid off took a deep whiff of the wine. I then allowed Goober to take a whiff. I then took a nip of it and handed it to him. He took a nip and declared, "Boy, that's good!"

It was good. We nipped on it and nipped on it. When we had finished about half of it, we started feeling it. We were one happy duo. Jokes and stories got funnier. Our legs got limber and we began staggering. Paul fell into the pond and crawled out on his hands and knees. We passed the jar back and forth, taking more nips. Then I fell in the pond. I just sat there in the middle of it enjoying the cool water. By the time I got out, the mud from the bottom was all stirred up and I knew the cows wouldn't drink it if they came up. I also knew that my dad wouldn't like that one bit. But who cared? By now, I certainly didn't.

We passed the jar back and forth until there was barely any wine left. By then Goober was so drunk that he could hardly stand up. But he talked bravely. In fact, that wine seemed to deliver courage right into both of our blood streams. Goober bragged that he would kick Jimmy Trubbel's ass if he showed up. I was getting braver. I agreed that I would kick his ass if he showed up, and Earl's too. In fact, we decided that we could and would kick the asses of everyone in the Trubbel family if they showed up.

Now you couldn't say ass in polite company in the Riverview community or around the house where the women were. You could say "butt." If you said "ass" at school, you would get your mouth washed with soapy water. If you said it at home you could get a switching. That was a hard one to figure out. At Sunday school, you could talk about Jesus riding into Jerusalem on an ass and use the word, too. A preacher could tell about Samson taking a jawbone of an ass and killing a thousand Philistines. It was right there in the Bible. But I was punished if I used it. There was another word you couldn't use in polite company, and that was, "piss."

You could say, "pee, or pee pee." But you couldn't say, "piss" without getting punished, or at the least scolded. But, Daddy could say these words and many more like them, or worse, when he was upset and receive no punishment at all. When Mama would scold him, he would say that there was nothing wrong with the words because they were both right there in the Bible. Mama's most profane words were, "Land of Goshen," and "Lawdy me." We children couldn't say damn, but we could say darn, dern, dat gum, and dang. We couldn't say, God, Christ or Jesus Christ, except with respect, or it would be taking the Lord's name in vain. None of us wanted to use the Lord' name in vain anyway. But we could say gosh, golly, gee whiz and jimminy cricket. We could say these derivatives or euphemisms with a clear conscience until some preacher came along and convinced us that using them was just as bad as saying the real thing. He said, "Saying Gosh is as bad as saying God, and darn was a bad as saying damn. They are all cussing." Thereafter, we had some guilt for just saying, "dang," "darn" or "gosh." We could say, "He let at toot," or "she pooted," but you couldn't say, "He let a fart." Fart was considered cussing by some and just plain course language by others.

I finished the last drop of the wine and passed out the creek bank. I don't know whether Goober passed out or not. Both of our clothes were wet and muddy. I knew I was drunk the first time I woke up. Then, every time I'd wake up I would say to myself, "The next time I wake up, I'll be sober." But, I'd wake up and still be drunk. The last time I remember waking up, I was looking up and seeing the face of James leaning over me. He shook me awake and then shook Goober awake.

"Boy are you guys in for it now," he declared. I tried to get to my feet: instead, I lunged headfirst into the pond again. Goober tried to get up, but couldn't stay up. Neither of us could walk. James climbed up the creek bank, waved his arms and yelled for Daddy. His yelling also caught the attention of Mary and Ruth. They all three came running down the watering pond to see if I was dead or what. When they came up and started gandering at us, I wished that I was dead. When they saw that we couldn't even walk, let alone walk a straight line, they began snickering at us. They thought we were funny, at the least we looked funny to them.

James declared that we were skunk drunk and the empty half-gallon fruit jar was the evidence to back up his statement.

I was in inner conflict. I was proud that I had been successful in making such potent wine. But I was filled with guilt and shame for being drunk. Dad dragged me to my feet saying nothing. With Ruth's help, he half carried me to the house. James and Mary were helping

Goober. Every few feet I would say to myself, "By the time we get to the next fence post, I'll be sober and Mama will never know." As we approached the barn, I thought, "By the time we get to the barn, I'll be sober and Mama will never know." When we got to the barn I said to myself, "When we get to the windmill, I'll be sober and Mama will never know." As we passed the barn, Mom spotted the two of us being half dragged up to the well. By the way we looked, she thought maybe we had drowned. She rushed down to the windmill to check on us.

When she got to the well, Dad said, "We've got a couple of drunks here. What do you suggest we do with them?"

"Lawdy mercy!" She exclaimed. "Well, get their dirty clothes off first and then put them under a cold shower."

We got our clothes off and James dipped cold water out of the keg of drinking water to shower us with. The cold water did seem to sober us up a bit. Dad saddled Tony up and put Goober on behind him and took him home.

I put on my other shirt and overalls and waited for James to bring the cattle up from the pasture for milking. I couldn't face my sisters or Mama that night. Tomorrow was Sunday and a revival was starting with a Baptist evangelist doing the preaching. I wondered how I was going to face Mrs. Whitley, knowing how much she hated alcoholic drinks of any kind, even if Jesus did turn water into wine. She taught my Sunday school class.

One thing was for sure: Baptist preachers could make you feel as guilty as sin itself. The question was, "Would Goober and I get religion and be saved from our terrible sin before the week was out?" If the Baptist preacher didn't convert me, another preacher would.

CHAPTER 10
THAT OLD TIME RELIGION

In the Riverview community if you believed that the Bible was the revealed Word of God, and you accepted Christ as God's son, didn't cheat or steal, didn't really get drunk, went to Sunday school pretty regularly and were willing to help your neighbor, you were considered a Christian. Pete Morris might have even been considered a Christian by some using that standard. While it was true that most families considered themselves members of different denominations, our community Sunday school and church were truly ecumenical. On Sundays, the adults and the children all studied out of the literature published by the International Sunday School Convention. The little kids had cards with a picture on one side with the memory verse under it. On the backside there was a golden text and a couple of paragraphs relating to it. Older kids had the same memory verse and golden text on a fold-over leaflet, with more paragraphs about the lesson. The adults had regular workbooks that they carried home to study next week's lesson from. At the end of the adult lessons, there was a list of questions to answer.

If you went into town, there was no single ecumenical group meeting. The Baptists, Methodists, Pentecostals, Church of Christ folks, First Christian Church members and others had their own buildings and their own doctrines. In town, you separated yourself from those who didn't see it just like you did. If somebody in any of these groups didn't see everything alike, then they'd split and start another group in somebody's home. The Christian Advents met in homes. They claimed it was the only Scriptural way to meet. They claimed the early church didn't waste money on buildings and if you were going to use the Bible as your guide and authority, you couldn't use the Lord's money on buildings. Strangely, every other church used the same Bible, and it allowed them to use the Lord's money to build church buildings. It seemed everybody could find their doctrine in the Bible. Some even claimed it didn't matter what you believed as long as you were sincere. However, they did their dead-level-best to get everyone to join their church.

The denominational walls in town were up and high. However, in the country the walls were down most of the time, or at least until revival time, or when a visiting preacher showed up to preach on a Sunday. We always knew which denomination he represented. Therefore, we knew in advance what doctrines he would emphasize. The schoolhouse was owned by everyone, therefore anyone's preacher was free to come out and preach.

There were more Baptists in our community than those of any other stripe. Naturally, more of their preachers or evangelists seemed to be invited to preach. At least that was the way it seemed to Mom and Dad. In fact, Dad said that the only thing growing faster than the Baptists in the whole state was Johnson grass. We were members of the Church of Christ, a denomination that claimed that it wasn't one. But in everybody else's eyes it was one.

When my dad tried to defend its doctrine on the subject, Marion Dobson said, "If you refuse to call a mule a mule and instead call it a cow, that doesn't make it a cow. Likewise, claiming that you are not a denomination by claiming to be something else, doesn't change the fact that you are one." That argument didn't quite convince Dad. So one Sunday Marion opened the big dictionary on the stand in the upper grade classroom and read the definition of denomination. He read that "The verb form, denominate meant to name and its noun form, denomination, meant something named, usually a church or religious organization." He then asked Dad right there in the front of everybody if the Church of Christ was named. True Whitely and Daddy, both members of the Church of Christ, had to admit to Marion in front of the whole assembly of Riverview folks that it was named, but they still weren't humble enough to admit that the Church of Christ was a denomination. They claimed you couldn't trust the dictionary on religious matters. Mr. Dobson ended the discussion by saying, "You men prove that I was right in using a mule in my original illustration." The whole congregation really got a big laugh out of that, but I didn't get the joke.

Marion loved to debate, and he could make any other preacher, or member of any other denomination, squirm when they tried to defend their peculiar doctrines. He concluded the discussion on the Church of Christ not being a denomination with this remark, "The members of the Church of Christ may not know they are a denomination, but everyone else does." Mr. Whitely got a little mad, turned red in the face and even threatened to take all the Church of Christ folks out of the Riverview Sunday school and start meeting with them in the Whitely home. But he didn't.

There was one practice that nearly everyone agreed to. That was baptism. The Pentecostals practiced immersion, as did the Baptists, the First Christian Church and the Church of Christ. The Methodists sprinkled their converts instead of dipping them. Strangely, at least it seemed to me, the groups who taught that Bible baptism was immersion couldn't agree on what its purpose was. Stranger yet, to me, was the fact that they all preached from the same Bible but baptized differently.

The Church of Christ and the First Christian Church claimed that you weren't saved until after you were immersed. They quoted Peter on Pentecost, "Repent and be baptized every one of you in the name of Jesus Christ for the remission of sins and you'll receive the gift of the Holy Ghost." They argued that this verse said that forgiveness came after you were baptized, and it was absolutely necessary to be baptized for forgiveness, or in order to, have your sins remitted and be saved. They stated that the apostle Paul was told by Ananias, "Arise and be baptized to wash away your sins." So it was very clear that you weren't saved before you were baptized or you could be saved in your sins. They then backed up their argument with a lot of illustrations from the Book of Acts and from the books written by Paul and Peter. They claimed that Catholics, Methodists and Presbyterians weren't really even baptized, or saved, since they were only sprinkled.

However, the Church of Christ and the First Christian Church never could explain to any other church's satisfaction, or even to their own members, what the gift of the Holy Ghost was that you received when you were baptized, or exactly what it did.

The Baptists and the Pentecostals argued that you were saved as soon as you received Jesus into your heart. They believed that you "Repented and were baptized because of the remission of your sins." They argued that "for" really meant "because of," not "in order to." In other words you were saved first and that your sins were remitted, and because they were forgiven, you repented and were baptized.

The Baptists had another twist on their baptism doctrine. They claimed you couldn't be saved out of the church and that you had to be baptized to get into the church. Moreover, you had to be in the church to get to heaven. But they claimed baptism still didn't save you. Yet, they were named Baptist, because they baptized all their converts.

The debates about Bible subjects would go on in homes, on street corners, under our mulberry tree and at revivals. The Baptists, Methodists and Pentecostals held revivals. The First Christian Church and the Church of Christ conducted gospel meetings, or protracted meetings. The Church of Christ reasoned that the true church of the Bible was alive and well, and that they didn't need reviving, because they were it. Others believed that all churches needed to be revived occasionally. They claimed that if the Church of Christ really believed what they preached, they couldn't sing a familiar song, that was sung in every church, "Revive Us Again." Church of Christ members didn't have an answer to that one either, but they kept on singing the song anyway.

The Church of Christ folks were the only ones in the community that didn't use the Lord's prayer in worship. They claimed it wasn't even the Lord's prayer. Rather it was the disciple's prayer, because Jesus gave it to them to use in prayer. Moreover, you couldn't pray, "Thy kingdom come" because the Kingdom had already come and the Church of Christ was it. But, they didn't object to their kids praying that prayer every morning after books took up in school. I concluded that it was because they didn't consider using it at school real worship, since we didn't have singing and the Lord's supper with it.

The Baptists and the Church of Christ had another strange twist on the Scriptures, they claimed that women were instructed to keep silent in the church, and were not to teach or usurp authority over men. Women couldn't be preachers, elders or deacons. They couldn't even read the Scriptures during worship services. Each church made a distinction between Sunday school and the worship services. During Sunday school, usually held at 10:00 A.M., you could sing and pray just like you did at 11:00 but that wasn't worship. Women could read the Scripture in front of the men and even argue her point of view at that time. When it came her turn to read the verse out of the Sunday school quarterly or out of the Bible, she not only read it, but was expected to teach the men and women present, what it meant. At 11:00 she was forbidden to even read the shortest verse in the Bible, "Jesus wept," in front of the same men and women because somehow at that magic hour, reading and explaining the Bible was no longer Sunday school but was a worship service. At that hour it violated the law on silence, teaching and usurping authority over men. My mom claimed that that didn't make any sense, but to the men in authority it didn't have to make sense.

At big Friday night dinner at our house there was a big discussion on the subject. My mom wanted Mr. Whitely, the Dobson brothers and my dad to show her why it was all right for women to violate the silence law by singing and making announcements at the 11:00 o'clock service but wrong to read the Scripture at the same service. She also wanted to know why women could read Scriptures at 10:00 o'clock and teach the men what they meant, but they couldn't teach the same thing to the same men at 11:00 o'clock? She wanted to know why it was usurpation of authority over men for women to read the Scriptures to men at 11:00 and not usurpation of authority when they read the same Scripture to the same men at 10:00? She said the Methodists and Pentecostals were at least consistent, for they preached that it was OK and they allowed women to participate in any service. She charged the Church of Christ and the Baptists with being both inconsistent and hypocritical on the subject. She said the men had made up a bunch of man-made laws on women that couldn't be found in or supported by the Scriptures or logic, and that they were totally inconsistent in applying those man-made laws.

She also wondered why the women at the Riverview Sunday worship services could read their verses, and teach the men what they meant when there was only Sunday school and no preaching, but were in violation of the silence, teach not and the usurpation laws, and when there was preaching. She asked, "Why did it become a sin just because a preacher showed up and preached?" None of the men could answer that one, either.

The First Christian Church even let the preacher's wife preach when he was away holding meetings, but the Baptists and the Church of Christ wouldn't have allowed a woman to say one word from their pulpits. Mama wanted to know where the women prophets in Joel's prophecy did their preaching. When she threw in the four daughters of Philip who prophesied, and the women in Corinth who were told to do their praying and prophesying in church with their heads covered, she stumped the men. Not one man could explain why God waved his magic wand at 11:00 o'clock and changed the status of both the women and the men. None of the men could explain why it was necessary for all the women, even the teen-age girls, to wear head coverings to services according to this same Scripture, but they couldn't preach or pray which the Scripture clearly allowed. Yet, it was clear that the Corinthian women prayed and prophesied right there beside the men in the same assembly.

Mama tried to get the men to explain why it was a usurpation of authority for women to wait on the table, and pass communion up and down the aisles, but wasn't usurpation to pass the communion trays right to left, along the pew. In fact, she asked Gilbert Dobson to show her from the Scriptures where passing the communion carried any authority to begin with. She said the men serving it couldn't make one person partake of it, nor could they keep them from partaking of it. "What authority do the men, while passing the trays, exercise?" she asked. He was stumped. But, he wasn't going to change his practice. She pressed him further, "You are a preacher in the Church of Christ, tell me what authority there is in wording a prayer?" She knew that there wasn't a Baptist or a Church of Christ preacher in the whole country who could answer those questions and remain honest, if they continued to defend their teaching and practices. I think Dad thought she was just about ready to cross the line on women exercising authority over men, as he saw it, but he couldn't stop her, because he had never been able to answer her questions either.

Members of each of the denominations had favorite Scriptures that nailed down and clinched their peculiar doctrines and practices. Some members parroted their preachers, and their preacher parroted other preachers, some even referred to the original Greek language to support their doctrines.

My dad said that not only did most of these preachers not know any Greek, they couldn't even quote the Greek alphabet. He said he knew as much Greek as most of the preachers knew. He said the alphabet started with Alpha and ended with Omega. Mama knew that too. She had attended Southeastern State College in Durant where our Uncle Tom Houston taught history. He had been superintendent of schools in Idabel before that. Mama had taught in the elementary school at Smithville before she and Dad were married. She didn't claim to be an authority, but she was totally confident in her ability to think logically, and she said that was more than lots of the preachers did. She was only one of two persons in the Riverview community who had gone to college. So, this sort of made her an authority. That's why she wasn't afraid to challenge the men about church doctrines. Most of the men who were running the churches didn't even have a high school education. Her final judgment on different churches was, "Well, nobody can be any better than what they have been taught. Therefore, we'll all have to rely on God's grace to get to heaven, not on our own smarts or good works."

The Pentecostals had revivals that caught the attention of everybody, or so it seemed. They often went by the name, Holiness Church. Nearly everybody called them Holy Rollers, but not to their faces.

When they held a revival, it was a sight to behold. Their preachers could get worked up as much as the black preachers who came to the little black church over in Texola. The Pentecostals were good. But the black preachers were still champions at putting on a show.

Most people would rather go to a black church revival than to go see Buck Jones at the movies. In fact, when they had a revival, there were lots more white folks in attendance than black folks. They held their meetings under a brush arbor in Texola. It was open on all the sides. White folks would stand ten deep around the arbor to watch and listen. The blacks would sit inside on wooden benches. You heard more amens during one service there than you would hear in most white churches in a year. When a black evangelist was preaching, he invited the "Amens." He said it was just like saying, "Sic'em" to a bulldog.

The Holiness preachers claimed that the age of miracles was still on, but most other preachers claimed that that age passed with the death of the Apostles. The Holiness Church passed out handbills all over town one week promoting its upcoming revival. The church announced that it was going to have a great faith healer, Billy Opery, come to town. He could heal the sick, had raised the dead, spoke in languages he had never studied and saved thousands of sinners. Miracles would happen, too, right before the eyes of true believers. Apparently Billy Opery was one of their biggest preachers.

One of our neighbor families, the Marshalls, were Pentecostal and they promoted this revival all over the community. Mr. Marshall rode up on a horse one evening and invited us to their revival. He claimed that this young evangelist, Billy Opery, had performed all manner of miracles, and we would witness miracles being performed every night. "So please come," said Mr. Marshall. Daddy said we would try to make it a night or two.

There was to be a singing group from Amarillo, presenting special music. A picture of Billy Opery was on the top of their handbills and a picture of this musical group and a five-piece band was on the bottom. The band had drums, a guitar, a mandolin, a clarinet and a fiddle. This was going to be a great revival. Mr. Marshall claimed that he had seen tumors come right out of people and roll around on the floor. He claimed to have seen goiters fly off people's necks and bounce on the floor. He claimed that Billy Opery had raised the dead and given sight to the blind, just like Jesus and the apostles did. No miracle seemed too great for him not to claim.

Mom and Dad discussed going to town and attending the revival one or two nights. Mom said we ought to go at least one night out of respect for the Marshalls. She said we would have to agree not to sing because of the instruments though, because this might offend the Whitelys. They, being members of Church of Christ, didn't sing with or use instruments in worship. They claimed that they sang a cappella just like the Apostolic Church did. Mr. Whitely reasoned that by our singing, accompanied with their instruments, would be giving instrumental music our approval and that would be a sin. But Dad put up a counter argument about it that went like this.

"There is nothing wrong with singing at their revival. If they want to use instruments, its their business. We won't be playing them, so why do you think it would be wrong?"

Mr. Whitely responded, "Because Brother Gilbert Dobson said so, and he proved it right out of the Bible. The New Testament says, 'Sing' and it doesn't say 'play,' that's why!" Dad closed the argument with, "Well, I don't plan to play, I plan to sing."

Gilbert was the eldest of the two Dobson brothers. He was converted in a gospel meeting of the Church of Christ when he was thirteen and went on to become a preacher in it. Marion, a year younger, was always competing with his older brother. He joined the Christian Advent Church about this same time and was later ordained in it.

They continued with their sibling rivalry through Bible arguments and debates for the rest of their lives.

Daddy told us a story about Gilbert and Marion one night after our family had our prayers. He was using it to teach Ruth about long prayers. She had just finished her prayer. She had kept on saying, "And, Heavenly Father," after each request of God. Then she paused after re-addressing God, as she thought of another request. She was spending more time addressing God than praying. It didn't look like she was ever going to say, "Amen." When she finally finished her prayers, Dad suggested that God might appreciate prayers that were shorter, since the Lord's prayer was pretty short.

To make a point about long prayers, Dad told about going home to spend that night with the Dobson boys, when he was boy. It was shortly after the two brothers were converted. Marion was Dad's age and Gilbert was one year older. It seemed that they had begun competing to see who was the most religious, the Church of Christ convert, Gilbert, or the Christian Advent convert, Marion.

They convinced their parents, who weren't all that religious, that the family should have a vesper service each night that included Scripture readings and prayers. The parents agreed to the evening service and told the brothers that they could conduct it. On the night that Dad spent with them, each of the brothers had set out to convince Dad that he was the most religious and the best Christian.

Each read a selection of Scripture and Gilbert, being the oldest began the first prayer and Dad said it went about like this. "Dear loving, gracious and all righteous Heavenly Father, we thank you for the food on our table. We thank you for our parents. We thank you for our home. We thank you for our daily bread and the butter and grape jelly we put on it. We thank you for the vegetables from the garden, the tomatoes, the okra, the beans and the radishes. We thank you for the fish in Turkey Creek and in the Red River. We thank you for the birds and the rainbows. We thank you for our farm, our school, our country, the rain, the sunshine, the Bible, and our neighbors. We thank you for the Church of Christ where all the saved are found." He had prayed on and on. Finally he was ready to conclude it with, "In Jesus name, Amen." He had thanked God for everything anybody could think of, but concluded his prayer by excluding Marion and the members of all other churches from the saved on the earth. Stealing all these things you could be thankful for first and leaving little to nothing for Marion to thank God for or pray for, was bad enough. That infuriated Marion. But, ruling him and the Christian Advent Church out of the saved on earth, infuriated him more. So he drew back his fist and punched Gilbert in the mouth just as he finished saying, "In Jesus name, amen." Their dad separated them. But Marion said Gilbert had no business using up all the things you could thank God for and leaving nothing for him to pray about. Moreover, he said he thought it was God's business to decide who was going to heaven and not Gilbert's or the Church of Christ's. After that, their Dad called a moratorium on vespers. He said he thought from then on, each one could go into his own closet to pray in secret, and allow God to do the open rewarding.

We did attend the Pentecostal revival in town one night, and it wasn't like anything we had ever witnessed at the Riverview schoolhouse in a Baptist revival or Church of Christ gospel meeting.

The band was loud and spirited. The local preacher was loud and spirited. Billy Opery was louder and more spirited than the rest. The congregation got in the swing of things. I say swing, because these Pentecostals were swinging and swaying. You could always tell Pentecostal women from the visiting women. They never had permanent waves. Rather, they combed their hair straight back and tied it in a knot on the back of their heads. They wore no makeup. Their dresses dragged on the floor. They did seem to dress modestly just like the

Bible taught. They wouldn't have dared to get a Boy Bob haircut, a haircut that left the hair on a woman's head just a little longer than a man's. They didn't drink, dance or smoke. But they did a lot of swaying to the upbeat music that Mama claimed was the same as dancing. She said later that the only difference in what they did and which people did at the Stumble Inn dance hall east of town, or at the Silver Slipper dance hall over at Sayre, was that they didn't dance with partners. Like all the fine Christians in the Riverview community, she didn't believe in judging others.

With the singing group and the band from Amarillo leading the way, the singing was about the best that I had ever heard. With the windows open in their building you could hear the music all over town. The visiting Methodists, Baptists and some of the Church of Christ folks, added to the volume and quality of the singing. Most Church of Christ members just listened but their kids were caught up in, and participated in, the singing to the displeasure of some of their parents. Dad sang out, too. It seemed to me though, that he did it to show True Whitely up, as much as he did to praise God. He wasn't going to let someone else's use of instruments determine whether he could sing or not. Moreover, he wasn't going to let someone else dictate whether he could sing or not.

When brother Opery got up to preach, his text was from Mark 16:17-18. "And these signs will follow them that believe; In my name shall they cast out devils; They shall speak with new tongues; They shall take up serpents; And if they drink any deadly thing it will not hurt them; They shall lay hands on the sick and they shall recover."

That sounded like gospel to me. It was pretty clear to me — right out of the Bible. If you believed, these things would happen. It was pretty clear to Brother Opery too.

"We believe, therefore, these and other miracles will happen, here and tonight," Brother Opery proclaimed.

Brother Opery preached on. He had a habit of making an emphatic statement, then he would make loud sucking noise as he drew in his next breath.

"Jesus raised Lazarus from the dead! Isn't that what the Bible says?" "Suuccckk!"

"Jesus restored the sight of blind Bartimeus! Did he not?" "Suuccckk!"

He continued, "Paul raised Eutychus, did he not?" "Suuccckk!"

Before long you just could hardly help being sucked up into the whole service.

He gave other examples of healing in the Bible and stated unequivocally that Jesus promised us the same power, if we truly believed. "He is the same yesterday, today and forever," he intoned. When he rounded out the sermon, he had an alter call. People were invited to come forward, confess their sins, repent, receive Christ into their hearts and get saved. He invited the drunkards and adulterers, the backsliders and the lukewarm. He was pleading. He was terrifying. He painted the picture of the saved in heaven walking on golden streets. He described hell filled with sinners, with its everlasting fire and brimstone, where the worm dies not and where its sinners gnash on each other with their teeth.

"You'll burn for eternity!" "That's an everlasting fire!" "Those worms are maggots and they'll eat away at your flesh forever and ever!" What preaching!

The people were invited to come forward to be saved and get the baptism of the Holy Ghost and fire. "The Holy Ghost will empower you with special gifts and the baptism of fire will burn away your lusts of the flesh: sex, liquor and coveting other people's property. It will burn away the lust in your goggling eyes for pretty women, and you will quit going down to the city swimming pool where lust was rampant among folks running around half naked. The movie house will close its doors when this community starts looking to heaven instead of looking at those damnable Hollywood pictures up on a silver screen. That Stumble Inn dance hall east of town, and even the Silver Slipper at Sayre, will also close their damnable doors if the town turns to Christ, because dancing feet and praying knees aren't found on the same legs. True converts will give up smoking, chewing and dipping tobacco. Moonshiners and bootleggers will go out of business. You'll quit swearing and using the Lord's name in vain"

"The guilty sinners are going to burn in hell. But, today is the day of salvation, so harden not your heart," he shouted and admonished with great fervor. "Don't provoke God!" He warned.

My guilt for making wine and getting drunk was almost overpowering. When I thought of the lust of my eyes in wanting to see TooWoo Tompson' silk panties convicted me more. He stopped the invitation song after each verse to convince and convict sinners who hadn't gone down to the mourner's bench yet. He walked up and down the center aisle warning, pleading and begging. By the end of the invitation song, a dozen folks had gone forward, most of them Pentecostals-people whom you'd think never had any lust of the flesh, or the eyes, by the way they dressed and groomed themselves.

Brother Opery asked the music group from Amarillo to sing the last verse again.

"Almost persuaded, harvest is past

Almost persuaded, doom comes at last,

Almost cannot avail, almost is but to fail,

Sad, sad that bitter wail, almost but lost."

That last verse did it. As he surveyed the crowd and he looked straight into my eyes. I could imagine him knowing every evil thing I had ever done. I was convicted, but the invitation song ended right there and it was too late to go forward, much to my relief. I wouldn't have to confess my sins and get saved before this group of people after all. Then to my dismay Brother Opery said, "Let's sing the first verse of one more song. We can't let any sinner go home unsaved and left on the road to hell tonight. What if you had an accident on the way home tonight and were killed? Where would you spend eternity? In God's heaven or in Satan's burning hell?" I didn't know how we could have an accident on the way home in a wagon. But he worked hard to convince the crowd that something bad could happen to them that very night. He not only implied that God could, but God would cause something bad to happen to the unrepentant.

"What if you had a car wreck on the way home and were killed?"

"What if your team ran away and scattered you and your family half-dead along the road?"

"What if you had a heart attack? Anything might happen to you and you would go into eternity unsaved and unprepared to meet your God. In the judgment the Lord would say, 'Depart from me, I never knew you.' "

"How about the last verse of *Sinners Jesus Will Receive*?"

They began singing, "Sinners Jesus will receive, even me with all my sin."

That half-gallon jar of wine and getting drunk kept passing before my eyes. TooWoo's panties crossed my mind. All those dirty four letter words I had uttered around other boys crossed my mind. Stealing the grape syrup for my wine crossed my mind. The beer keg crossed my mind. Lying about the French harp and the candy bar crossed my mind. These and a dozen more sins crossed my mind. I was a sinner. If I died tonight on the way home, I was going straight to hell. There was no doubt about it.

"Purged from every spot and stain, heaven with him I enter in."

Brother Opery shouted during the song, "Today is the day of salvation. Harden not your heart. Don't be guilty of hardening your heart. God is merciful to sinners."

"Sing it o'er and o'er again, Christ receiveth sinful men."

"Come to Jesus," Brother Opery pleaded.

"Make the message clear and plain."

He looked right into my eyes. The Holy Spirit must have enabled him to see right into my heart. He must know all my sins, just like God knows. He knew about the wine, the beer, the cussing, TooWoo's silk panties, the stealing, the lying and all the rest of my sins.

"Christ receiveth sinful men."

Before they could start the last line, "Sing it o'er and o'er again, Christ receiveth sinful men," I was totally guilt stricken and under conviction. I rushed forward and grabbed Brother Opery's hand and he shouted, "Praise the Lord. There is more rejoicing in heaven tonight over this one sinner who has repented, than the ninety and nine in the fold."

This sinner had repented. There would be no more cussing, smoking, drinking, stealing, or lusting. Even though I had only gone to four movies, two of them Shirley Temple ones, I would gladly give them up too in order to escape hell. I was struck on Shirley Temple, but she couldn't be the one for me because she tap-danced, and Brother Opery stated clearly that genuine Christians didn't do any kind of dancing, because all kinds of dancing are condemned in the Scriptures.

The meeting was just beginning. People came forward to pray these sinners through. Two grown folks, whom I didn't know, came up and wrapped their arms around me and began praying for me. The preacher came over and laid his hands on my head and shouted for God to baptize me with the Holy Ghost and with fire. I didn't feel the Holy Ghost or the fire. I did feel Brother Opery's sweaty hands. I was crying though. I decided that the Holy Ghost must have broken my heart when it baptized me and the fire was burning away all my lusts without my knowledge.

There was a rather large woman standing in front of the pulpit with her hands outstretched toward heaven and she was speaking in an unknown tongue. There were two men standing right behind her. Brother Opery came over and laid his hands on her head, pushed and she fell backward into those men's arms. She didn't fall forward. She didn't fall sideways. She fell the way she was supposed to, right into those two men's arms. As she hit the floor, the big electric fan on the platform blew her dress up. I nearly lusted with my eyes again, right there in church just after getting saved.

Brother Opery shouted, "Another saint slain in the Spirit!"

He then announced that anyone with a sickness or an affliction was welcome to come down during the prayer of the sick. A number of people came forward claiming a variety of health problems like an ulcer, backache, headache, rheumatism and sprained this or that. But no one had come forward yet with a big tumor in their gut, a crippled leg, deaf ears or blind eyes. Bertie Wilson was there and she had a big goiter on her neck. She then went forward to be healed. I was hoping to see her goiter pop out and bounce on the floor just like Mr. Marshall had testified about. I wondered if it would be red and bloody, maybe like a pig's heart looked at butchering time. But it didn't pop out and roll on the floor.

There were about ten people speaking in tongues. Others were praying over the sinners who came forward. Others were praying for the sick folks. Dad came up and took me by the arm and said, "It's time to go before they start rolling on the floor." We went out to the wagon and started home. No one said much, at least about my conversion. I guessed that they were happy that I had finally decided to quit my sinning to follow Jesus, even if it was a Holiness preacher who converted me.

The next day I was in one field plowing maize, and James was in another field plowing cane. It was so dry. There hadn't been any rain in a month. The maize, cane and cotton were wilting. At breakfast, Dad said that if it didn't rain in the next few days, we were going to lose the whole crop. That frightened and saddened all the family. If there was no rain and the crops failed, we couldn't pay the bank loan made on this year's crops or the loan on the mules. We couldn't meet the mortgage payment on the farm that came due the first of every January. The thought of giving up, having to sell out and going to California saddened us more. Dad said that we were not the only ones in the same pickle. Everyone else was, too. So as I plowed, I thought about God, sin, forgiveness and the power of Holy Ghost.

I had heard all those people speaking in tongues last night, but God hadn't seen fit to give me the gift of tongues, no matter how hard those two men had prayed for me. I thought, maybe you had to help the Holy Ghost along if you were going to speak and pray in tongues. So I began jabbering some language like I had heard in church the night before.

It was in the middle of the morning and a few clouds were in the sky. I was sure that I was asking God to send rain by speaking in my newly found tongue. I believed that the Holy Ghost would cause it to rain. "And these signs will follow them that believe," the preacher had said. Jesus himself had said it! By the time I plowed a half-dozen more rows, the clouds were gathering thicker and thicker. And, they became blacker and blacker. I began speaking in my unknown tongue without stopping.

It started to sprinkle. God had answered me by my speaking and praying in that unknown tongue. Hallelujah! Hallelujah! I unhitched the mules and headed them for the barn. It was a race with the rain. James was also bringing his team in from the cane field. By the time we got under the shed beside the barn, it was pouring down. We unharnessed the horses and went to the house after the rain stopped. James said that we must have gotten at least a half an inch and if we got another one like it, the crops would be saved. I asked him if he knew why it had rained.

"Because the clouds came up, of course!" was his answer.

"No it wasn't. It was because I had prayed in an unknown tongue for rain and God answered my prayer."

I felt both thankful and little superior to the rest of the family. I thought I probably had an inroad to God that the rest of the family didn't have. He answered my prayers, and hadn't answered theirs. And, just maybe that no one else in the community had what I had, because of my baptism by the Holy Spirit.

I was kind of afraid to say much about the tongues, because no one in our family believed they were real. I would have to admit that I had been skeptical too. I wondered about the prayers of those men who prayed last night that I would be baptized with the Holy Ghost and fire. Everyone who knew anything about the Holiness churches, knew tongues were the sign that all of 'em got when they were baptized in the Holy Ghost. I noticed that the only people who went forward and got the baptism of the Holy Ghost were Pentecostals. There wasn't one Baptist, Methodist, Christian Church or Church of Christ member who had received it and spoke in tongues.

I knew that I wasn't actually given a gift to speak in tongues, at least not consciously. I knew that even today out in the field, I had made up the ones I spoke. But they worked, didn't they? I wondered if God was a respecter of persons, even though the Bible said He wasn't. He had given tongues to those Pentecostal people last night but I wasn't sure He had given me the gift. I was in a quandary. Did I have the gift of tongues, or had I prayed in tongues just because I wanted to claim God gave me the gift of tongues?

James was pleased that I had prayed and that it had rained, whether I had the baptism of the Holy Ghost or not. If my conversion last night and my prayers in tongues today caused God to send rain, that was OK with him. Mom and Dad had already decided that we wouldn't go back to the revival again. They reasoned that if it did me some good-then that was fine. They were even glad that I had been converted. It might just mean that the mulberry tree would survive after all. If James were converted, it would surely mean its survival, because it would have enough limbs left to survive. But, there were just too many differences in what we believed and what Pentecostals believed for us to continue to support their revival.

By the next day at noon, the rain had soaked into the ground enough for us to resume plowing. There were still a few clouds floating by. On my second row, I started my speaking in tongues again, hoping that I was going to get that other half-inch of rain we needed. I jabbered and I jabbered in my newfound tongue. I didn't know what I was saying, nor could have anyone else. Every time I saw a cloud approaching, I would start speaking in my unknown tongue. The clouds kept floating on by. I finally gave up.

At the supper table at nights, following our going to the Pentecostal revival, we discussed the event. No one made fun of my conversion but they all had doubts about the tongues and healing parts of the service. We really wanted to see brother Opery go out to the cemetery and raise the dead like Mr. Marshall said he could. Dad also noted that he didn't take a swig of poison or pick up any rattlesnakes like the Bible said he could. Dad had already had that discussion with Mr. Marshall. But, he had explained that that would be tempting God and that Jesus clearly taught that you shouldn't tempt the Lord your God. Daddy asked why wouldn't praying for the sick be the same. Wouldn't that be tempting God to put up or shut up, too? Mr. Marshall had no answer for that.

Whether I had been baptized with the Holy Ghost or not, I would forever be a changed person. Brother Opery's preaching had convicted me about sinning and the need to live a holy life. I would ever be grateful to him for that, because I would think twice before yielding to temptation after that one sermon.

I did have one malady that I wished Brother Opery could have laid his hands on and healed. It had caused me much embarrassment all my life and it would be especially so at summer school.

CHAPTER 11
MY ULTIMATE EMBARRASSMENTS

It seemed that I was born with weak kidneys and a weaker bladder. For as long as I could remember, I had wet the bed occasionally. Mom and Dad had rules at our house that pertained only to me. I wasn't to drink a second glass of anything at supper. I could not eat watermelon after mid-afternoon. Regardless of how late it was, before we went to bed, I had to go outside and pee. In the wintertime, I could use Mama's slop jar. But regardless of the weather or other circumstances, I had to go pee before going to bed. None of my other brothers and sisters had to. This was a rule that applied only to me.

It was also a rule at our house that James and I had to take our turns at taking two water buckets to the well at night and bringing them back full. Between the house and the well, there stood the little chicken house. Every night the chickens would climb up on the roosts to sleep. Unless they were disturbed, they hardly made any noise when we passed by on the way to the well, except for a few clucks. If disturbed, they could make a lot of noise.

It was known that occasionally some farmers lost chickens to chicken thieves. The thieves seldom, if ever, tried to steal chickens from farmers who had dogs. Dogs could hear the faintest sounds, and would bark like the devil when anybody came around. So, if you were going to steal chickens, you wouldn't pick anyone with dogs to steal from.

It was also known that coyotes, on occasion, sneaked into a chicken house and made off with a chicken. It had happened to us one morning. Just as Dad got up to go outside to pee, the chickens started squawking. A coyote came out of the chicken house and was dragging an old Rhode Island Red hen by the neck. Dad grabbed the shotgun fired it at the coyote that had already dragged the chicken past the windmill. The coyote dropped the chicken and ran off. Things like that always brought such a commotion among the other chickens, that it would awaken the entire household. That old hen the coyote dropped was dead and we had fried chicken that night for dinner.

The very possibility of either event happening made the trip to the well after dark frightening. In order to reduce my fear, when it was my turn to go get the water, I whistled all the way to the well and back. I always propped the back screen door open so I could run up the steps, out of the darkness and into the kitchen when I got back to the house. On occasion the wind would blow the screen door shut, and I would spill half the water getting in and away from any boogy man that might be behind me in the dark. This always meant another scary trip to the well to replace the water I had sloshed out of the buckets.

One night, when it was my turn, I went to the well as bravely as possible. I was whistling while I worked. Going by the darkened doorway of the chicken house was the worst part of the trip. The doorway didn't have a door on it. It was just an opening. Behind the opening was total darkness. Some of the old hens would cluck quietly as I passed by. Their clucking was a little bit comforting. It seemed that the hens knew if it was a family member who walked by, or if one of us even entered the chicken house. The clucking would get a little louder if one of us stepped in but it was hardly enough to notice. The dozen or so steps of the trail beyond the chicken house to the well, and the fresh water keg, were taken without any light from the kitchen door. Their location put you out of sight of the back door after you passed the chicken house. This was where you had to be the bravest. On this night, as always, I sucked up my courage, whistled, and walked very briskly in those last steps to the water keg. Then I heard all the chickens start clucking in unison, but not too loudly. However, it put me on full alert.

I filled the buckets and started to the house. I was giving a side-glance through the door into the darkness of the chicken house as I passed by. Suddenly, there was the loudest squawk I ever heard. I threw the buckets down, spilling the water. I charged the back screen door so hard that I nearly knocked a hole right through it. It must have blown shut and I was screaming for someone to open it up. I had yanked the handle off the door trying to get in. Dad rushed out to help. He found me frightened out my mind, yelling and clawing at the screen door.

On this night I would not have had to go outside to pee. I had peed in my pants trying to get the door open. I blamed my wet over-alls on the spilled water. About that time, James came in, folding over, and busting a gut with laughter. He was laughing so hard the tears were streaming down his cheeks. He had sneaked out, closed the screen door, gone into the chicken house and yanked an old hen off the roost just as I walked by the chicken house door. He nearly scared me to death. Everybody thought it was a pretty funny trick — even Mama. They got just about as big a laugh out of the trick as James did. He wasn't punished, but was warned by Dad not to repeat it. However, he did have to go to the well and bring fresh water to the house every night for the rest of the week.

This event illustrates how easily I wet my pants and the bed. At school, we raised our hands and extended one finger if we wanted to go get a drink. We extended two fingers if we wanted to go to the toilet. Mrs. Brooks knew of my lack of bladder control and always gave me permission to go the toilet between bells.

When she was sick, she usually asked her brother to substitute for her. He was a bit gruff, and didn't respond well to the hand signs when you wanted to go out for a drink or to the toilet. He had already decided that most of the time kids just wanted to get out of the classroom to fiddle around unwatched.

When books took up after the morning recess, I realized that I should have gone to the toilet at recess. But I thought I could hold it until noon. But, about the middle of the period, the urge hit me hard and then got worse. I held up two fingers and the substitute teacher didn't even notice me. I clicked my fingers to get his attention. I was still ignored. I clicked my fingers louder. I waved my hand. I did everything but shout to get his attention and permission to take care of increasingly big problem.

He finally acknowledged my hand sign, but he shook his head, "No!" I was in a crisis. Should I bolt out of my desk, make a run for the toilet and maybe get a switching for doing so? Or, should I just sit there and hope I would make it until lunch. I decided the switching was not the better alternative. So I just sat there squeezing and unable to concentrate on any schoolwork.

Finally, I had to let it go. It soaked my pants and the pee ran down the back of my seat, where it dripped down on Bernelda Dobson's shoes. When she realized what was dripping her shoe, she let out a bellow and had a wild-eyed fit. That sure got the substitute teacher's attention that my hand signals had failed to get. Not only did she get pee on her shoes, but, there was a pretty good sized puddle forming on the floor under our desks. I wasn't going to be blamed. The teacher came up to scold me, but when I told him it was his fault, he backtracked. He sent me out to the closet in the hall to get some newspapers to wipe the puddle up. In my mind, he should have been the one who had to wipe it up, not me. He caused it. I had to wear wet pants the rest of the day. All the boys teased me without mercy about the dark wet spot on the bottom of my britches.

The only good thing that came out of this accident was that the substitute teacher started paying attention to the hands that went up, especially the ones that held up two fingers on them.

On another occasion, a similar thing happened and my embarrassment was even greater. Huck Jones was still the most popular boy in the entire school, in spite of his lack of loyalty. His cowboy boots, his paint saddle horse, and his Red Ryder BB gun made him the choice for a friend by every boy, and nearly every girl in school. I courted him regularly, in spite of him laughing his head off at my fright when Jimmy confronted me down at the river that time.

One Monday night, he invited me to spend the night with him. We had a project we were doing for our geography lesson and the county demonstration competition. We were going to build a volcano and actually have it erupt, smoke and all. If we did it right, we believed it would be the best demonstration project in school. We then would automatically be entered as a home demonstration project in the county competition at Sayre. The County Agent had visited our school a few days before and said the school's best demonstration could be entered in the county competition. He said the demonstration could be about anything we were studying, or about anything that would help farm families live better. We set our sights on winning the blue ribbon for the best project in Beckham County. He also said that the best three demonstration teams would get their pictures in the *Beckham County Democrat*.

When we got to Huck's house after school, we saddled his pony and went to the river bottom to drive their milk cows in. We stopped at the Buchannon farm to get a drink. Mrs. Buchannon invited us in for a piece of cake and short visit. We obliged her. The Buchannon farm had a big clay pit that the WPA workers took wagon loads of clay from to build up the roads. When the weather was dry, the clay was nearly as hard as concrete. When it was wet, it was slicker than snot. We told them about our project and asked if we could take some clay from their pit. They told us to take all we wanted. When we got the cows in the cow lot, we went down the clay pit and brought back a couple of gallons of red clay.

After the chores were done that evening, we went into the house for supper. Boy, did they have a treat, Kool Aid. Rare was the occasion for the Rowland household to have it to drink. But, the Jones family drank it all the time. And, you were permitted two teaspoons of sugar in it if you wanted.

After supper Huck and I began working on our volcano. We put a heavy piece of cardboard on the table and formed a volcano about twelve inches in diameter at the bottom and about ten inches high with a hole in the top about an inch wide. It looked a bit like a clay teepee. We used some chicken wire to reinforce the clay. When finished, we set it on the shelf above the stove to dry and harden. It was going to take a few days for it to dry enough to be ready to load for an eruption.

After a few games of checkers we were ready for bed. I told Huck that we ought to take a leak before going to bed. I was full of orange Kool Aid. We did, and when we came back in he put me on the back of the bed that was shoved right up to an open door. There was no full moon that night. Had there been, the dark clouds overhead would have hidden it. About three o'clock in the morning I was awakened. There was some thunder and lightening. But that is not what awakened me. I had wet the bed. It had soaked the bed sheet and mattress about a foot in from the edge. But, I was saved, or at least I thought I was, by the storm that was brewing. It started raining and Huck was sleeping soundly. How was I going to be saved from the embarrassment of wetting the bed? The rain was going to rain in through the screen door and soak my side of the bed. That's how.

As the rain started running off the roof, I would open the screen door and catch water in my hands and throw it on the side of the bed. When the growing wet spot from the rain reached the wet spot where I had wet the bed, I felt safe. I woke Huck up and made him move over. I told him the rain had blown through the open door and soaked my side of the bed. He moved over and we both went back to sleep.

At the breakfast table the next morning I told the Jones that the rain had blown through the door and soaked the bed on the side I was sleeping on. Mrs. Jones said she would take the sheets off and dry them out during the day. I had successfully covered my accident. I was home free! No one would ever be the wiser!

Huck and I joined the crowd of kids on the way to school that morning at the corner near his house. We told about our volcano and how it was going to win the blue ribbon at the county seat competition. That school day went along as usual.

But the next morning, as Goober and I approached the Jones' corner, there were fifteen or twenty kids waiting by the mailboxes. I thought this was unusual. Usually the kids were strung out for a half-mile, divided into groups of two to five kids. This morning, something in the air was definitely different. When we got right up to them, they started a familiar chorus. I had heard it lots of times, but it had never been directed at me like it was that morning by nearly half the kids in school.

"Two little boys lying in the bed,
one turned over
and the other one said,

Bob Rowland, you peed in my warm place.

Ha, ha, ha, ha."

Huck was leading the chorus. He was a dirty traitor. Yesterday he was supposed to be my friend and today he has rallied nearly half the school to mock me. He had to be the one to tell them that I wet the bed at his house. But, how did he know, I wondered. Singing their little chorus once wasn't enough to give them satisfaction. They had to repeat it a half dozen more times as I tried to run on ahead of them to school.

Goober lagged behind and asked Huck what the deal was. Huck said his mom had taken the sheets off the bed to dry them out and discovered two separate wet spots. The one nearest the center of the bed was a yellow one and the outside one wasn't. So she concluded that I had wet the bed and had tried to cover it up.

Now, I was disappointed in Huck, and Mrs. Jones. She shouldn't have told on me to Huck, and if he were a true friend, he would not have told about my peeing in the bed to the rest of the students.

Wetting the bed was not the worst accident I ever got into, though. One day I got home from school ahead of the rest of the kids. I was prowling around the kitchen cabinet looking for something to eat. On top, next to the box of Hershey's Cocoa and Dad's Honest Snuff jar, I discovered a flat box of Ex Lax. I had never seen it before and had no idea what it was used for. Out of curiosity, I opened the box and found wrapped in tinfoil, a bar of chocolate that looked about like a bar of Hershey's chocolate candy. It was divided into little squares just like the Hershey bars were. I broke one off a little square and tasted it. It didn't taste quite like Hershey's candy, but it was the best thing this side of town when compared to anything else there was in the house to eat. I finished one square and it was obvious now that the bar had been tampered with. So, I broke the rest of the squares on that one side to balance it out and ate them. I hoped that Mama or Daddy might not miss any being gone with the sides all even.

I didn't mention my discovery to anyone. I figured I had a good thing going and would eat a little of my find each evening until it was all gone. I would have candy and no one else would. I would face the punishment later on, if there was any punishment. The pleasure of the candy now surpassed any punishment I might have to experience at a later date anyway.

As usual, I went to the river bottom and brought the cows home the first thing after school. Then I helped James cut and split enough wood for the night. After it was cut and split, we would go to the barn and feed the livestock, milk the cows and slop the pigs.

After the rest of the chores were done, James got an armload of wood first and started for the house. I knelt down and filled my arms with the rest of the wood. When I started to stand up, lifting the load of wood, without any notice, I suddenly messed my pants. I had the runs. I dropped the wood and called for Mama to come here fast. She came down to the woodpile and wanted to know what my trouble was. She thought I might have cut my foot with the ax. I told her in hushed tones that I had messed my pants. So she said she would put some water in the wash tub on the back porch and for me to go up there and get my pants off.

I walked kind of spraddle legged to the porch and took my clothes off. It was pretty bad. No, it wasn't pretty bad. It was terrible! I really had messed myself up. But I bathed and Mama rinsed me off with warm water right out of the teakettle. She brought my other pair of pants to put on and wear the rest of the evening. Everybody in the house learned what had happened, though they did not know the cause. I was terribly embarrassed.

After dinner that night, we four older kids were doing homework around the table by the light of a coal oil lamp. I finished mine first and it was my turn to get the water for the night.

I took the two water buckets, got the water and brought it back to the kitchen. We always set the two, two-gallon and a half buckets on a bench that was almost shoulder high to me. I always set one bucket down while I lifted the other one, with both hands, up and on to the bench. As I lifted the first bucket, I had another accident.

Mama was sitting at the end of the table reading the *Women's Home Companion* with baby Rick in her arms. I sidled up to her to get her attention. But, she didn't pay me any attention. I nudged her and quietly pointed down to my pants, hoping she would understand that it had happened again. She still didn't get my message. I supposed that she was used to the smell of Rick's dirty diapers and couldn't smell me.

Mary caught on fast. She sniffed and shouted, "Puuwee!"

She then looked at me and noted my embarrassment. She pinched her nose and shouted, "Oh no, not again!"

Everybody looked at me, sniffed, grabbed their noses and then scattered from the table.

I took another trip the back porch and my second bath of the day. There was no way for me to go to school the next day, because I had messed in both pairs of my pants. Now, they were both dirty. I did put on a pair of James' old overalls. They were way too big, but by rolling up the legs and cinching the shoulder straps as tight as I could get them, I could wear them. The next day it was my job to wash both pairs of my dirty pants and dry them.

Huck and I finished our volcano and it was time to demonstrate it at school. We had it all worked out. We would cut open one of Huck's dad's shotgun shells and put the gunpowder in the bottom of the volcano. Then we stuffed it with torn up scraps of asbestos from an old stove protector. We would mix a little sand in the asbestos to make it look real. His dad had about six feet of fuse that was left over from road job he worked on with the WPA. They had blasted some big rocks, using dynamite while putting in a bridge.

Mr. Jones said that a foot of fuse would be plenty to give us time to get out of the way of the eruption. We carried our volcano to school and were ready for the competition.

Taylor Comstock and Jimmy Trubbel entered the contest with a demonstration of making grasshopper bait mixed with poison. Etta Boyd and Bernelda Dobson entered lye soap making project. The rest of the kids were content to let one of us represent them at the local and maybe the county finals.

It was ladies first. The two girls brought some lard, lye and other stuff that they mixed together, heated and poured into molds to make bars of lye soap. But, they spilled some of the mixture on the teacher' desk. Then they turned the can of lye over on the desk, where it started eating at the varnish. They didn't even get to finish their demonstration because Mrs. Brooks stopped it to clean the greasy crud and lye off the desk.

Taylor and Jimmy brought a paper bag full of wheat bran, a bottle of syrup and some baking soda to put on their grasshopper poison demonstration. Before they started, Mrs. Brooks had decided to spread newspapers over the top of her desk before their demonstration started. They were going to mix their concoction in a wash pan. Taylor was going to mix while Jimmy gave the spiel. Taylor dumped all the bran in the wash pan at one time and it was running over. He had brought a big wooden spoon to do the mixing with. As Jimmy explained that you added the syrup to the bran and it would attract the grasshoppers, Taylor poured syrup over the pan full of bran and then started mixing it. The pan was too full and the gooey mixture also started running over on the teacher's desk. Jimmy then explained that you then added arsenic to the mixture and it would kill the attracted grasshoppers. Taylor took a tablespoon full of Arm and Hammer baking soda, representing the arsenic, out of the soda box and sprinkled it over the bran and syrup mixture. Jimmy said that when it was well mixed you scattered it all around your garden or field, and it would kill off all the grasshoppers that had been feeding on your crops or vegetables. The wash pan was running over and Taylor was mired in a sticky mess. Jimmy said you could use sawdust instead of wheat bran as your base, but bran would be better. By now the kids watching were snickering again as the pan ran over on the teacher's desk. Mrs. Brooks also stopped their demonstration and asked the boys to clean up the sticky grasshopper bait that now pretty well covered the newspapers on her desk.

Huck and I both narrated the story of how volcanoes formed, what set them off and what happened when the erupted. We explained that their ash was sometimes blown miles and miles into the sky and that it settled miles and miles away, often adding valuable nutrients to farm soil. As Huck finished his final spiel on volcanoes, explaining their positive and negative aspects, I lit the fuse. We backed away and covered our ears as the fuse burned toward the base of our volcano. No one but the teacher knew that we were going to have a little explosion. Mr. Jones had assured her that there wasn't enough powder from one shotgun shell to worry about. But, Huck and I kept our hands over our ears anyway and waited.

The powder ignited with a soft boom. It gave a good puff of smoke. The asbestos mixed with dirt erupted out of the top of our volcano. The asbestos floated down and made a perfect demonstration. Our volcano was judged the best demonstration project of any class at the Riverview School. We were going to Sayre.

One week later, we were in Mrs. Brook's new Plymouth on the way to the county competition. The three of us were riding in front seat and the volcano was sitting on the back seat. We were determined to win a blue ribbon and get our pictures in the *Beckham County Democrat*, published by Mr. O. R. Wilhelm. Mrs. Brooks had drilled us on our spiel and we had it down perfectly.

There was one change in our plans that we didn't tell the teacher about. We weren't quite pleased with the eruption at school. It was more of a puff than a boom. Our geography book said that the sounds from erupting volcanoes could be heard for miles around. It said they rumbled and roared. Ours didn't rumble or roar. We decided that there wasn't enough gunpowder in our volcano. If the powder from one shotgun shell made a small puff and shot the asbestos and sand up two feet high and for two feet around its base, the powder from three shells would make a rumble and roar. That would really impress the judges. So, we had cut three shells open, put the powder on a sheet of paper, rolled it up like a fat cigarette, stuffed our fuse in one end, and taped it tight. It looked like a big white firecracker and was thicker than a thumb. We placed it inside the volcano and taped the other end of the fuse to the corner of our cardboard base. We were ready.

The competition was held in the Beckham County Court house. The county courtroom was where the finalists were to demonstrate. Mrs. Brooks, Huck and I watched other demonstrations and kept whispering to each other that ours was better. Finally, we were called.

One judge announced that Huck Jones and Bob Rowland, representing the Riverview School, would demonstrate the value of volcanoes to world agriculture. We put our volcano on the table in front of the courtroom and Huck thanked the honorable judges, other worthy competitors, and guests for the opportunity to participate in this countywide competition. We made our well-rehearsed spiels and proceeded to light the fuse. We then stepped back and waited for the eruption. The fuse burned kind a slow but once it burned under the edge of the volcano, we knew what to expect.

Well, there was an eruption. In fact, it was probably the biggest explosion in the county since some fishermen got caught blasting the fish out of a big water hole on Red River near Sayre with ten sticks dynamite a couple a years ago.

Everyone expecting a puff of smoke and little bits of asbestos and dirt to shoot out the top, was in for a surprise. In fact, discovering that three times as much gunpowder as used before would cause such an explosion surprised the dickens out of Huck and me. What we got was very different than what we expected.

There was a rumble and a roar. But before the rumble and the roar there was a big boom. The rumble came from chunks of hardened clay hitting the ceiling, the walls and even the windows. Some chunks rained down on the audience. The roar came from the gasps of the honorable judges, other worthy competitors and the invited guests. Bits of asbestos filled the air. Some people were choking and scrambling toward the exits. The sheriff's office was on the same floor. He and a deputy came running in. The county clerk followed. The county treasurer ran in with a fire extinguisher. Someone had already called the Sayre fire department.

Huck and I were bewildered. Could that little amount of gunpowder really make that much noise and send that many chunks if clay flying through the air? We knew right then that we, and others who were watching our demonstration, would have a newfound respect for the power of a real volcano.

The county agent was trying to explain to the sheriff what had happened. Huck and I just stood there afraid to speak or move. Everybody in the courtroom was gasping for breath. We heard the siren of the fire truck coming. By the time they arrived in front of the courthouse, we sensed that we might be in real trouble.

The photographer from the *Beckham County Democrat* had arrived and had unpacked his camera just before we started our demonstration. He was there to photograph the winners. His first photo, as the dust, smoke and asbestos settled, was of Huck and me standing behind of the remains of our volcano.

The pictures of the red, white and blue ribbon winners were on the back page of the *Democrat* the next week. Huck and I had our pictures in the front page. We were shown examining the mangled and twisted chicken wire that we had used for reinforcement.

Our picture was right beside one of Governor Alfalfa Bill Murray. Governor Murray was making fun of President Roosevelt's plan to plant windbreaks of millions of trees on a strip of land a hundred miles wide from the Dakotas down to and through Oklahoma. Governor Murray was quoted as saying, "This plan is like sowing hair on a bald head. It will never work."

Mama was so proud of our picture alongside the Governor that she tacked that front page on the wall next to the kitchen cabinet, and it stayed there until we left for California.

Huck and I denied using any more gunpowder than was in one shotgun shell. Mrs. Brooks confirmed that the same demonstration a couple a weeks ago had gone off safely and without a single problem in the Riverview schoolhouse.

Huck and I would always have the honor of blowing up the Beckham County Court house without even getting arrested. We were often referred to as "the dynamite twins" when seen together.

Since not many of my ventures went like the last one, I was determined to make a success out of at least one. I was going into business.

Chapter 12
The Entrepreneur

When school was out for cotton picking the next fall, I was determined to work hard and save my money. I knew I'd have to buy my own school clothes and winter pair of shoes. But once those were bought, I'd have the rest of my money to do anything I wanted to with. We didn't really pick the cotton, we pulled the cotton bolls. There was never enough rain anymore to fully mature the cotton, so the bolls never fully opened to make it possible to pick the cotton out. We took the cotton to the gin and their machines opened the bolls and extracted the cotton and cotton seed from them. The going rate of pay for pulling bolls was twenty-five cents for every hundred pounds you pulled. On an average day, I could pull about one hundred and fifty pounds. On a good day, in tall cotton, I might pull two hundred pounds. I made about two-dollars and a quarter a week. The cotton picking season lasted eight to ten weeks every fall. A hard working fourth or fifth grader could make as much as twenty-five dollars during the season. I was in the fifth grade now. Daddy, during the hardest times, took half of what we made to pay family bills.

After our clothes were bought, some of our extra money was spent for Christmas presents. Hardly any was ever saved, because there was so little to save. We did most of our buying through the Sears-Roebuck and Montgomery Ward catalogs. We never said, Montgomery Ward. We called the store, "Monkey Ward." It usually took about ten days for an order to turn around and be delivered to our mailbox. On the eighth or ninth day after mailing our orders, our excitement level always reached a fever pitch. We would watch for the mailman from the cotton field. He usually arrived around eleven-thirty. If we saw Mama carrying in a package from the mailbox, we would drop our cotton sacks, no matter where we were on our rows, and high-tail it to the house. Opening these packages was the high-light of the cotton-picking season.

When my school clothes were bought and delivered, I had around seven dollars to spend anyway I wished. I decided that I would become a door-to-door salesman. The Cloverene Salve Company was always advertising for representatives to sell their salve. It was supposed to cure just about any external disease or skin sore. It was good for cuts, bruises, pimples, boils, risens, eczema, chapped hands and lips, bunions, corns, and all other skin ailments. I sent in a penny post card and asked to represent them. They wrote back and told me I would have to order at least six cans of their salve in a starter sales kit. I could start with a dozen. I chose the six-can order. My cost would be thirty cents a can, and I could sell it for fifty cents. I sent them two dollars and ten cents, and that included postage and handling. My cost was going to be thirty-five cents a can.

The sales kit arrived just before Christmas. This meant that I would be free on Christmas break to go door to door selling this miracle salve and make some real additional pocket change. I might even have to order a refill by the first of the year.

It was a cold December day when I took my sales kit and headed down the road to make my first stake outside the cotton patch. The first house was the Buchannon's.

Mr. Buchannon was a tall man, polite and was a fine farmer. He had the finest team of mules in the community and he had britchen harness for them, too. Britchen harness was the complete harness with brass knobs on the hames, brass rivets holding the leather traces together and brass fasteners on the check lines. No team in Beckham County looked better than Mr. Buchannon's.

When I knocked on his door, he welcomed me in. I really didn't have my spiel down at all. But, I told him that I was selling Cloverene Salve. It was the best salve made by any drug company and would cure everything from bunions to pimples. It would also protect cuts and bruises from infections.

He had two daughters who were out of school but still living at home. When I mentioned pimples, one of the daughters came into the room and examined my product. I was using one can for demonstrations and that left only five to sell. She ran an index finger across the salve, sniffed it and rubbed it on the back of her other hand. I could tell she liked it. She also had pimples. The only other thing on the market that claimed to cure pimples was Fleishman's Yeast. It didn't take me long to give them the price of my salve.

Mr. Buchannon asked her what she thought. She said she liked it. He pulled out his pocket book, took two quarters out, and I had my first sale. I thanked them, picked up my sales kit, ran out the door and jumped off their porch heading for my next sale. I had made nearly fifteen cents in profit already. The next house was the Morris's. I didn't think they had the money to buy a can of my salve, but it was worth the try. They had forgiven me for cutting Joe up, so they let me in. But, they said, "No," to my sales proposal. I went on to the Jones' and made my pitch. They bought. But, it seemed more like it was out of kindness than need. I didn't care why, I just hoped everyone would buy a can, whether it was out of kindness or not. No one else seemed to be so kind though. I spent the rest of the day knocking doors up and down country roads and did not make another sale. I arrived home, with my sample can and three full cans in my kit. Counting my postage and handling and the cost of materials, I had walked nearly ten miles and had earned a net of thirty cents. One good thing happened though. The Boyds invited me to have lunch with them when I got to their house. And I got to sit by Etta as we ate.

Mama suggested that I take my sales kit to town the Saturday before New Year's day. She said other peddlers did so, and if adult peddlers could sell on the street, surely it would be OK for a boy to do so. I took my kit to town the next Saturday and opened it in front of the Farmers' Bank. I didn't know most of the people going up and down the sidewalk. Most of the Riverview folks who came by had already said no to my pitch. I offered my wares to everybody who walked by. Some of them politely listened, but only wished me luck. One woman said that she still had nine cans of the stuff in a dresser drawer at home that she would sell to me for ten cents a can if I sold out. That wasn't the most encouraging news of the day. I stood there on the corner for three hours, from eleven until two, and had sold only one can of the salve. I was cold and shivering. I gave up and put my kit in our wagon. Goober and Taylor came by a half a dozen times to see how I was doing.

It was obvious, I wasn't going to get rich selling Cloverene Salve. In fact, I still had two unopened and unsold cans of the salve when we finally left for California.

As soon as I abandoned my spot on the street corner, I looked up Goober and Taylor. We had a couple of hours left in the day before the drawing, and nothing in particular to do.

The agent who ran the Rock Island train station was there every morning until the eleven o'clock passenger train came in from Amarillo on its way to Oklahoma City. After loading and unloading the freight and the luggage, and taking care of the passengers, he headed home for lunch. There was also a four-thirty passenger train that came in, heading west for Amarillo every day. The agent usually came down to the station around three-thirty to open up and prepare for its arrival.

There was a black water tower next to the station about twenty-five feet high, and it was about twenty feet in diameter. It had a ladder that started from about six feet off the ground and went to the top. There was a clearly posted sign with bold letters in white paint under the last step of the ladder that read, "KEEP OFF." Such a prohibition, combined with the natural curiosity of nine and ten-year old boys, made the sign a challenge. I had fifty cents in my pocket from my only sale that day. I was going to hold on to it.

The three of us walked over to the cotton gin and jumped around on cotton bales for fun. The cotton gin was just a few yards from the station's water tower. We sat down on a bale of cotton and took in our surroundings. The sign on the water tower became an immediate challenge.

I said, "You guys are too chicken to climb that ladder and take a look in the water tank."

They responded, "So are you."

"I piker either one of you to," I replied.

"We piker you to," they challenged.

"You are both fraidy cats," I charged.

Nearly anyone could get any boy to do nearly anything, even dangerous things, by pikering him or calling him a fraidy cat. Our pride was at stake when we were so charged. My piker and fraidy cat charges were not going to work that day. I would have to think up a better motivation.

I thought of a plan that would make nearly any poor boy do a dangerous or prohibited thing. I would bribe them with money.

"I'll give either one of you who climbs to the top a nickel," I offered.

"I would, but about the time I got to the top, the agent would show up and I'd probably go to jail," Goober replied.

"No you won't! They wouldn't put you in jail for that, and the ticket agent won't be here for another hour at least," I argued.

I pulled out a buffalo nickel to temp them.

"It'll buy a Mr. Goodbar. It'll buy a Coke or a Delaware Punch. It'll buy you a hamburger at Aunt Carrie's," were my tempting offers. Goober just couldn't resist any longer.

"I will if you guys lift me up to the first rung on the ladder and keep a lookout for the ticket agent and Elmer Renner. I don't want no town marshal showing up about the time I get to the top," he said.

That was a deal. We walked to the water tower. After looking around for Elmer Renner, any of our parents and the ticket agent, and seeing none of them, we lifted Goober up on our shoulders. He grabbed the bottom of the ladder and pulled himself up. He was in a hurry to reach the top, take a peek inside and hurry back down. When he got back down to the bottom of the ladder, he jumped to the ground. Suddenly he was sort of a hero to us and he was a nickel richer. He was pretty proud of himself.

Taylor suddenly got interested in climbing the ladder.

"Does the offer still stand?" He asked.

Reluctantly, I agreed to give him a nickel, too. We boosted him up and he went to the top in a hurry. He got back to the ground in good shape without being caught and arrested.

They then accused me of being the one who was a real chicken and a fraidy cat to boot. I could not be ridiculed, so I let them boost me up. I climbed up the ladder and to take a look. The top three or four rungs were pretty scary but I made it. I looked down into the water and thought that this tank would make a great swimming tank in the summer time. I worked my way back down and found that it was scarier than going up. I jumped to the ground and we skoodad-dled out of there. We stopped at Aunt Carries and all ordered a ham-burger. I also bought a Delaware Punch that I shared with them. I still had thirty cents from my sale.

As soon as we had finished the food and drink, we wandered off toward the ballpark. Some of the town folks were passing us on the way to Main Street for some Saturday visiting and to then wait for the weekly drawing. On our way, we passed the water tower. It looked like it must go up a hundred feet in the air.

On a clear day, you could see it before you got half way to town. It had a cyclone fence six feet high around it and two strands of barbed wire around the top. We looked at the fence and the tower a bit, and then I decided to make the best offer of the day.

"I'll give either one of you a quarter if you'll climb over the fence and all the way up to the water tank," I offered.

They mused over the offer, and I knew that Goober wanted that quarter. Taylor did too, but not as much.

"After all, the town's water tower wasn't much different than the water tower at the train station. It's just a little bit taller," I encouraged. "A whole lot taller," was Goober's response. "But, how will we get over the fence?"

That statement gave me hope that he might take the challenge. We didn't have a ladder. If we tried to boost someone over the fence, they would tear up their britches on the barbed wire. We decided to inspect the fence and the locked gate protecting it. We quickly dis-covered that the fence was tied with pretty heavy wire where it was fastened to the steel posts that the gate and lock were hooked to. It took only a few minutes to unwind that wire and get a small opening next to the ground. We pried the fence back at the corner and got a hole about big enough to crawl through.

There was a narrow ladder on one corner of the steel tower that went all the way to the top.

Goober looked up at the tower and at the gap in the fence corner. I took out a quarter and let him look at it.

"Feel it," I offered. He felt it and agreed to crawl through the fence and climb the tower. His agreement to do so really boosted Taylor's and my respect for him. If he really did it, we would actually admire him. When school started the next week, he would be the talk of the school. This could be the bravest exploit of the year. We looked all around and didn't see a soul ready to ask us what we were doing. We knew that anybody who could walk would already be downtown jawing and waiting for the drawing. Elmer Renner would be standing in front of the Dixie Store in his ten-gallon Stetson hat and his cowboy boots, along with the men. The women would be gathered in front Pucket's Grocery store and the movie house. We decided to do it — that is, Goober decided to do it. After all, wasn't he the only one who had enough guts to climb the railroad's water tower first? Taylor and I were chickens. Goober was the brave one. We bragged on him. "Goober would take on King Kong if he met him." "Goober isn't afraid of anything or anyone." "You are the king of the mountain."

We couldn't wait much longer. It was nearly four o'clock, and after the drawing everybody would be loading up in their wagons and going home.

"Go on Goober. Do it and you'll have a free quarter," Taylor said.

I flashed that quarter. Goober dropped to his hands and knees and crawled through the fence as we held the corner back. He grabbed the sides of the narrow ladder and started up. When he was about twenty feet up, he looked down with a big grin on his face. We were clapping and praising him. Our clapping and praise encouraged him just like those amens did that preacher in the black church in Texola. The preacher would get louder and louder, Goober was getting higher and higher.

"You're doing great, Goober." "Keep going." "Keep climbing," we encouraged.

Goober must have climbed seventy feet in the air before he started looking down and looking real scared to boot. We were yelling "Go on the top or you don't get the quarter." But Goober had lost his nerve three-fourths of the way up. We would order him on up and he would not even answer. He couldn't even get one foot to step down one rung on the ladder. He started crying. We felt sorrow for him, but we didn't encourage him to come back down. He looked frozen — not just because it was so cold, but he was frozen to that ladder with fear. He was afraid to go up any more, but even more afraid to try to take a step down.

I felt sorry for him, but not too sorry to shout, "If you don't go all the way up, you don't get the quarter."

By this time, Goober wasn't interested in a quarter, or even a hundred dollars if I had offered him that much. If he had a hundred dollars, he would have gladly given it to anyone who could get him off that tower.

He could see the large gathering down town on Main Street. Mr. Ray, who owned a grocery and hardware store, was standing on someone's wagon bed in front of his store. He was turning the barrel that held the tickets. He was about to select someone out of the crowd to come up and pick out the winning tickets. Apparently, he spotted Goober three-fourths of the way up on the town's water tower. He pointed at Goober and asked the crowd what that kid was doing on the water tower, and whose kid was it?

The people all turned to look, and half the men and all the kids in town that Saturday started running toward the water tower. Mr. Ray announced that the drawing would have to be delayed until the town got that boy off the tower. With this announcement, everybody else in town rushed to the tower. Goober was getting his time in the spotlight. When Taylor and I saw the first men running in our direction, we started running in another direction, toward the wooden fence that surrounded the ballpark. We would hide there and watch what happened through the cracks in the fence.

We were close enough to hear the men yelling at Goober. "What are you doing up there? Come on down!"

About this time Elmer Renner came up in his Stetson hat wearing his well-shined black cowboy boots. He commanded, "Now, boy, you come on down here. Do you hear me, now? You've broken the law. Can't you read? This sign says, 'Keep out'."

By this time, the whole town and all the country folks had gathered around. Mama said later that you would've thought that the people were out to see Goober dive to his death. Or, they were acting like it was some final circus stunt that was going to be performed by the way they were all gawking. She thought they ought to be ashamed, standing there and gawking at that poor kid. Of course, she was standing there gawking, too. But, since she was a neighbor of Goober's, it wasn't gawking, it was showing neighborly concern.

One of the gawkers was Mr. Powers. He told Elmer that that was his boy he was talking to. He agreed to make him come down. But no amount of talking by the law or Mr. Powers was going convince Goober to let go of his grip and come down by himself. The men realized that Goober was scared to death and that he would not come down without some assistance up on the tower. In the meantime, Taylor and I had joined the hundreds of gawkers.

It was decided that Erick's football coach would go up and pry Goober's fingers loose and help bring him down. The coach was the best-muscled man in town. He was weight lifter and had played football at OU. He climbed up the ladder. When he got to Goober he tried to coax him to take one step down at a time.

The more he coaxed, the louder Goober screamed. He was not

going to let loose of his hold on that leg of the water tower. The audience became so quiet that you would have thought you were at a funeral. Half the people had at least an index finger in their mouths and were nearly biting them off. The rest were chewing their fingernails into the quick.

The coach realized that Goober was not going to come down voluntarily. If he tried to force him down without any safety gear, they might both fall to their deaths. He called for a pulley and rope. Some of the men ran down to the hardware store and brought back a big spool of rope and a pulley. Charlie Reynolds volunteered to take the pulley up and pull up the rope with one end tied around his waist. He said he had climbed and topped lots of tall pine trees in Colorado at the CCC camp. He was strong and fast. He took three short ropes up to use as safety ropes, or to tie Goober up if they had to. Well, they had to. They hooked the pulley onto a steel cross-brace above Goober's head. Then they ran the long rope from the big spool through it. They then tied Goober up with two of the safety ropes after prying his hands loose. To me, he sort of looked like an Egyptian mummy. It was a delicate operation, but they finally got him swinging free and the men on the ground began to let him down gently.

One great roar went up from the crowd when it was clear that Goober was going to get down safely. No hot shot fullback on Erick's football team had ever heard such a roar when he scored a touchdown. When the coach got to the ground he declared that he could win state if he had that kind of spectator support.

Goober didn't have to go to jail. He did make the *Beckham County Democrat*. He would have preferred getting there some other way. I thought he deserved the quarter and gave it to him, even if he didn't get all the way to the top.

Since selling was not going to be my way of getting rich, maybe there was a way of doing it without having to convince someone to buy my product. So, I ordered four steel traps from Monkey Ward. They were fifty cents each, and with the postage and handling, the bill came to two dollars and thirty-five cents. When they arrived I had the spots already picked out where I was going to set them along the river. Watch out Mr. Skunk and Mr. Opossum, because here I come.

Daddy told me that I would have to boil the odors off the traps before I set them out. He suggested that I throw in a few pieces of tree bark to help. Otherwise, he claimed, no varmint would come close to them. I boiled my new traps in the old iron wash pot with a few pieces of cottonwood tree bark thrown in. I saddled old Tony and was off to the river bottom to make my fortune. I had saved a syrup bucket full of rabbit and chicken guts to use for bait.

I set each trap in a hole in the bank of the river. I put a handful of stinking guts in the back of the hole and put the trap in the opening. The trap was then covered lightly with grass and leaves. I stacked a few limbs from nearby trees in the form of a V. Any animal going to my bait would have to step across my grass covered trap to get to the bait.

I could hardly sleep that night. I dreamed that I caught a skunk or an opossum in every trap. It was reported that big skunk hides were bringing up to a dollar fifty when shipped to Monkey Ward. Opossums were bringing up to a dollar. Those traps were going to be such cash cows that I could forget my failure at making money selling Cloverene Salve.

The next morning I was up and awake before anyone. The only cow I had to milk was Old Sway. I grabbed a milk bucket, rushed to the cow lot and got my milking done before anybody else was even awake. I took the milk to the house just in time to see Mama getting up to start the breakfast fire. I told her I was off to inspect my traps. She wished me luck.

I bridled Tony and riding bareback, headed for the riverbank. I rode up to my first trap and there was nothing in it. The second trap was also empty. By now I was already regretting spending the money I had saved on steel traps. I figured they would wind up like my Cloverene Salve, stored on some shelf. When I approached my third trap, Tony threw up his ears and got pretty excited. When the trap site came into view he reared up and nearly threw me. I then saw the prettiest sight, outside of maybe Etta Boyd or Sybil Hunter, I had ever seen. There was big black skunk in my trap with white stripes running down its back. I tried to ride Tony closer, but he wouldn't budge another step. I dismounted and tied him up to tree limb. You could smell the skunk spray strong now.

As I approached the skunk, it would turn its bottom to me and throw up its tail. I knew what that meant, and I wasn't about to get sprayed by a skunk, even for a dollar fifty hide. I had failed to take into consideration how I would remove the varmints I caught from the traps. I wasn't afraid of opossums, but skunks were an entirely different matter. I had to get close enough to knock that rascal in the head and then remove it from my trap. But every time I got close, it would throw up that tail ready to spray me. I picked up some big clods of dirt and threw at it, hoping to stun it enough to run up and knock it in the head with a stick. But I wasn't that accurate and the clods weren't that hard, anyway.

I decided that I could pick up enough old dead roots and short limbs from the trees to cover it, and once covered, it couldn't raise its tail and spray me. I started gathering loose roots and limbs and throwing them from a safe distance at the skunk. The plan worked. Before long I had that skunk loaded to the ground under a stack of wood. It couldn't move or raise its tail. By this time, the whole area was saturated with skunk odor and Tony was really getting nervous. I still had to get to the skunk and expose its head enough to kill it. I also had to check my other trap, get home for breakfast, get washed and off to school without being tardy.

I approached the skunk with great caution. It was so pressed down with pieces of wood that it couldn't move. I held it down with one foot on the woodpile as I carefully removed the sticks over its head. When its head was sufficiently exposed, I took a heavy stick and knocked it in the head. Gradually, I removed the other wood away and exposed the entire dead skunk. Boy, it was a beauty. I guessed it would probably be worth two bucks at the least.

I took it by the tail and started toward Tony. He wasn't about to let me, or the skunk, get close enough to ride him. He began to strain at the bridle reins. He started rearing up and jerking. It was not going to be the skunk and me and Tony going back to the house together.

The closer I came to Tony, the more he tried to break away. When I got within about ten feet of him, he lunged backward with such force that the bridle broke and he turned and hightailed it to the barn. Dad had just arrived at the cow lot to start his milking when old Tony came running up to the barn without a bridle on. His first reaction was to assume that the horse had thrown me, and I was probably lying on the ground somewhere, and maybe hurt. So, he put another bridle on Tony and raced down to the river bank to find me. I had already started home with the broken bridle, and was carrying my catch by the tail. Just as they came around a thick clump of bushes, they ran right into me. Tony reared up and threw Dad off. He hit the ground with a loud thud. He had his breath knocked out and couldn't even speak. Tony turned and ran back to the barn, dragging the reins under his feet.

When Daddy finally got his breath back, he looked at me and said, "You and those damned traps." Then he saw my skunk and his attitude changed. He was pleased that I had achieved some success in my latest venture. He did not appreciate the stench of skunk scent that, by now, had saturated my clothes and my skin.

We walked home, and by the time we got to the barn, everyone

We walked home, and by the time we got to the barn, everyone was up and doing their own chores. When I took my prize to the house, Mama refused to let it or me come in. She demanded that I take my clothes and bathe with soap and water on the back porch. But the skunk odor couldn't be washed off or away. Even lye soap didn't help. I put on my other change of clothes and was permitted to eat breakfast. However, no one wanted to sit next to me. On the way to school Goober wouldn't walk closer than ten feet of me.

When I arrived at school, the stench was still so strong that the kids all shied away from me. When books took up, the Miss Prock, my fifth grade teacher, decided that my stench so bad that I should go home for the day. I had no objections to that. Moreover, that would allow me the opportunity to check my last trap and skin my skunk.

I went home and checked my last trap. To my surprise and great joy, there was a big opossum in the fourth trap. What a success!

When I returned to the house with my second catch, Dad said he was real proud of me. He suggested that I cut all the fat off the skunk's carcass and skin and render it. He said that Mr. Hood at the drug store might buy the skunk oil. He said that he used it to mix some salves with. I felt sorry for anyone who would have to use it.

By the time I had skinned the skunk and cut away all the fat, I was used to the smell. I took a coffee can and put the fat in it and built a fire to render it. When finished, I had nearly a half-pint of skunk oil. When I skinned the opossum, I learned that it had more fat on it than the skunk did. I figured that if the druggist would buy skunk oil, he would buy opossum oil. So I rendered the opossum fat and now had nearly a pint of oil to sell.

This trapping business was going to be a great one. With the skunk and opossum pelts going to Monkey Ward and the rendered fat oil going to the druggist, I would be in the chips. When I took the oil to the drug store, Mr. Hood told me he no longer used varmint fat in his concoctions. So, all that rendering effort was for nothing.

Daddy suggested to Mom that we bake the opossum and see if it was really edible. He said that lots of people ate opossum. She reluctantly baked it for supper.

After school we did our chores, and I proudly told about my trapping venture. When I multiplied two varmints a day times sixty days left of winter months, when the pelts were prime, I was going to be the richest kid in school since TooWoo Tompson moved to California. At supper Mom placed a big baking pan in the middle of the table and Dad started cutting up the opossum. The meat smelled not just greasy, but it had an unusual and somewhat unpleasant odor. We ate wild rabbit and chicken all the time, but they were always cut up and fried in pieces. It became obvious to the other kids that this was not rabbit or chicken. Mary was especially suspicious. When she forked a piece and put it in her plate, she asked what it was. Daddy said it was Mississippi rabbit. She knew about jackrabbits and cottontails, but she knew nothing about Mississippi rabbit. Finally, everyone had a piece of Mississippi rabbit on their plates. I watched as each of the girls tasted Mississippi rabbit with reluctance. The rest of us ate a few bites. James hadn't taken a single bite, not even a nibble. Then he spilled the beans. "You're eating opossum!" That's all it took. The girls started running for the door gagging. Dad, Mom and I were determined to finish our Mississippi rabbit. James still had not even touched his. Daddy asked him why. He told the story of crossing Joe Van's pasture where one of his horses had died and was decaying. He said he went over to check it out with his nose pinched. He had noticed something moving next to it. He said it turned out to be an opossum eating on the dead horse. That's when Dad, Mom and I joined the girls outside. We were not just gagging. We were puking. So much for thinking that anyone could enjoy eating opossum.

My gallon of chicken guts didn't last long as bait on my trap line.

But, I learned that these varmints didn't mind eating on the carcasses of their cousins and siblings. As long as I caught something, I would have plenty of bait to continue my venture.

I spent the hour before milking time for the next two months setting, resetting and baiting my traps along the river banks, creek banks and the river bottom. I kept losing school days when I caught skunks, because the teacher would not allow me to come to school stinking. My Mom assured Mrs. Prock that I would do all the necessary make-up work and the regular homework under her supervision. That was agreed to, and I continued my great venture. Mrs. Prock, however, thought I would be better off with fewer skunks and more days in school. But Dad was on the school board, so she didn't object to my absences too strongly. Fortunately, I scored high enough on the achievement tests that everyone concluded that I was none the worse for my trapping venture.

I shipped my first ten pelts in a tow sack to Monkey Wards, in late January. It contained four skunks, five opossums, and one civet cat. On my birthday, January 29, I received a check from Monkey Wards for $14.60. It was the best birthday I ever had. Every kid at home and at school was envious. When I reported my earning to Mrs. Prock, she said, "Well, getting up early to run your trap line proves that the early bird does get the worm." I could envision wearing cowboy boots, a cowboy hat, a beaded belt and a shirt that laced up the front just like Tim McCoy and Buck Jones wore while chasing down outlaws. My final sale brought in only $5.30. I had a profit of $17.05 and the steel traps were still as good as new.

This was going to be the best winter I had ever had. But I didn't know that the next winter was going to be the worst. The summer of 1936 and the following winter would be the changing point in our lives. There would be no WPA camp money, no barbering money and very little money from pelts. There would be no money left over from cotton picking after our school clothes were bought. All winters were long, cold, windy and dreary.

There were three things that even made the last one in Oklahoma worse than the rest. They were the next Christmas itself — the itch and the lice.

The summer before that last winter was so disheartening. The crops that the drought didn't kill, it seemed that the grasshoppers ate. What the grasshoppers didn't eat, the dust covered and strangled.

One summer day Dad, James and I were chopping the weeds out of what cotton we had left that was still alive. The sun was hot and the weather was dry. It was about two in the afternoon we heard Mama calling from the back porch of the house, and waving a white dishtowel to get our attention. Dad knew something was wrong, so we dropped our hoes and ran to the house as fast as we could. Mom met us at the pigpen, and told Daddy that the old sow wasn't breathing. He grabbed a slop bucket and ran to the well for some cold water. He ran back and doused her good. But, she didn't move. He crawled over the fence and tried to arouse her. It was useless. She was dead. He told James to run to the house and bring the butcher knife. The old sow was pregnant and was almost ready to deliver a litter of piglets. James returned with the knife and Dad ripped open her stomach, hoping that he might still save the baby pigs. It was a cesarean operation. There were ten little pigs, perfectly formed in the old sow's womb, with hair and all. But, like her, they were all dead. Gone was the money Dad paid for the sow. Gone was the cost of feeding her. She had been dead too long to take a chance on trying to butcher her for the table. The meat would have spoiled anyway. Gone were the eight piglets that we could have sold for three dollars a piece at weaning time. Gone were the bacon, ham and sausage we would have had from the two we would have kept to raise, and butcher for ourselves.

Mama said, "I told you that you should have poured some water in that pigpen to keep her cool but you wouldn't listen."

That remark was more than Daddy could take. He began to shed tears. He was also angry. He wasn't so angry at Mom for her remark. He was angry at himself. In spite of Mama's pleading for him to do so, he had resisted pouring water in the pen at noon every day.

He always told her, "If I start it, I'll have to do it every day. So, I'm not going to start it." He didn't and we paid a great price for his not starting it.

Mom still had her garden and the fruit trees had some fruit. Mom knew that she and the girls would be able to can green beans, butter beans, corn, beets, tomatoes, pickles, and okra. Maybe not as much as we would need to get through the winter, but enough to help. We were living off the garden during the summer and she hoped to still have enough left over to can for the winter. She and girls worked the garden nearly every day, even carrying water from the horse tank to keep the plants alive. She was sure the apple, peach and pear trees would also bear enough to do some canning from.

We prayed for rain and it didn't come. We waited, we worked and we watched. One day when we were chopping cotton it finally clouded up. We were going to finally get some moisture. We left the hoes in the field and headed for the house. The wind hit just as we got to the yard. The wind kicked up the dust and the dust preceded the moisture. The moisture came, but it wasn't rain. It came in the form of hail. The chickens headed for the chicken house. The first hail stones were marble sized and they got bigger. Some were the size of baseballs. The ground turned white and then the storm was over. We kids ran out with wash tubs and collected two tubs full of hail. We could make ice cream. We were happy.

Suddenly, our happiness turned to sorrow, and the best ice cream in the world would not bring the happiness back. Mama had gone into her garden. The plants were stripped of their limbs, leaves and fruit. The vegetables were smashed and mashed into the ground. The fruit trees were stripped of their leaves and most of their fruit. The apples, pears and peaches that remained on the trees was hail damaged, and would never fully mature. There would be no canning this summer. The shelves along the wall of the storm cellar would be empty as we headed into the winter months. Only our potatoes could be harvested along with a few radishes. That was it.

Daddy had nothing to say as Mom returned to the house, and sat at the table with her face in her hands. He put on his hat and headed for the field to see how much damage the crops had suffered. Some crops had escaped the path of the hailstorm but when he came back to the house he estimated that a third of the cotton was destroyed. It was going to be a bleak year. The oldest kids could feel it about as much as Mom and Dad. We did make a gallon of ice cream that day, but its pleasure was bittersweet.

The grass in the pasture, where the horses and cattle grazed, was eaten down to the dirt. When there was nothing else to eat, they would graze the grass down far enough to get the roots. In doing so, they were picking up lots of sand with each nibble. The sand did two things, it wore the animal's teeth out and they ingested lots of it. This sanding, as we called it, was especially prevalent in horses. One of our horses, a pregnant mare named beauty, was sanded. She got down and could not get up. Dad used twist tobacco as a remedy to make her bowels move. He forced her to drink medicine the druggist recommended. He used a long neck beer bottle to get it down her throat. But, it was to no avail. Her bowels were so compacted from the sand that she died in the horse lot and had to be dragged to the backside of the pasture to decay. Now we had two and half teams to farm with, not three.

The cotton that remained had only two or three bolls to the stalk and the stalks were barely knee-high. We were going to have to really bend our backs while pulling bolls this fall.

We were so busy with our problems of trying to salvage something out of our crops and garden, that we completely forgot to meet the relief truck when it came to Erick on the day Beauty died. Our cupboards were really bare. The truck, however, was to return to Texola the next day. So Dad saddled old Kate and sent me eight miles over to Texola to get our food. I took two tow sacks and brought them back full of the same things that we usually received. There was one new addition that we had never seen before. They distributed a dozen artichokes to each family.

When I got home and we spread the supplies, Dad asked, "What on God's earth are these things?" Mama knew and she cooked half of them for supper. Daddy said that he couldn't understand why God created these artichokes or why anything but pigs would try to eat them. But, we didn't even have a pig, so we tried to eat them. Mom was the only one who acted like she liked them, or was getting anything out of eating them.

So went our summer and the fall didn't look much better. We all wondered what fall and winter had in store for us.

CHAPTER 13
THE COUNTY FAIR

No happening in our lives was more important than the annual Beckham County Fair each fall. It was a time for a break for two days from picking cotton and going to Sayre to see all kinds of competition. The women brought cakes, pies, cookies and competed for ribbons in baking. They also brought fruit jars filled with every kind of fruit and vegetable. Table after table in the Home Demonstration tent held Beckham County's best cooking, canning and sewing projects. The 4-H girls came with their projects right along with their mothers. If the mother or the daughter entered as many as three contests, they were confident of getting at least one third place white ribbon.

The FFA and 4-H boys brought their calves, hogs, chickens, dairy and beef cattle to the competition. Those who didn't have family or close friends near Sayre had to go home each night. The 4-H and FFA boys usually stayed in the stock barns with their animals for the whole fair and slept on piles of hay next to their animals.

If you didn't have a car, you hitched a ride with someone else or you didn't go to the fair from Erick. On Fridays they had the judging of most projects in order for the winners to show off their ribbons on Saturday when everybody with transportation came to the fair. But it was just too far for most folks to go with a team of mules or horses by wagon.

James had bought a little white bull calf from Mr. Jackson in November and prepared all year to take it to the fair as his 4-H project.

He broke it to lead by halter, and trained it to hold its head high and stand with its legs well spread. In addition to grass and hay, he had fed it a supplement of wheat bran and shorts. He took a curry comb and groomed it. He washed it down with soap and water. When dry, the calf's hair would curl and by nearly everybody's judgment in the Riverview Community, it was going to be a Champion, Reserve Grand Champion, or Grand Champion of the whole fair.

There was a joke in the community that everybody told and retold about shorts, a cattle and pig feed product of ground wheat. It went like this, "Did you hear about the farmer who went to the store and asked the storekeeper for some shorts for his hogs?" "Nope." "Well," the storekeeper said. "You farmers are really getting sophisticated. Today it's shorts for your hogs. Before long you'll be ordering brassieres for your cows."

Mom had some half-gallon jars of fruit she was going to enter. The county Home Demonstration Agent wanted all projects by women to be at the fair by Thursday. This way all the visitors could get to "ooh" and "aah" over their fine work for the rest of the week.

Dad was off working on some WPA project and wouldn't be home until Friday night. He left it up to Mom and James to get the calf to the fair.

Mom had arranged with a neighbor, Othello Martin, to get her fruit jars and the calf to the fair. He was one of the few people in the community that had a running car with a trailer hitch and a stock trailer. He planned to go to the fair for three of the four days. He would enter his wife's canned goods and her chocolate cake. She was a pretty fair seamstress and was also entering a winter coat she had made.

He took the women's entries down on Thursday morning and would return to hitch up the trailer and take James' calf early Friday morning in order to get it there in time for the judging.

On Friday morning we were up at daylight. We slopped the hogs, fed the horses, milked the cows and filled all the buckets in the house with fresh water. We then waited for Mr. Martin to arrive. The calf was standing beside our front door with its halter on. James was holding the lead rope, anxiously waiting for the trip to the fair. Eight o'clock came and we saw no sign of Mr. Martin. Eight-thirty came and still no Mr. Martin. James was really getting fidgety and Mama was getting angry. She knew they had to leave the house not later than nine o'clock to get to the fair in time for the cattle judging. At nine o'clock we saw the dust flying nearly a half-mile away. We squealed in delight as his black 1931 Model-A Ford pulled up on the road in front of our house.

When Mr. Martin drove up, he realized that there wasn't enough room to turn the car and trailer around in our front yard. So, he decided to back the trailer across the bridge covering the bar ditch beside the road and then back it down lane to our house. In other words, he would back the trailer to the calf instead of letting the calf walk to the trailer. Big mistake!

Running late and in the rush, coupled with his inexperience in backing a trailer behind a car, he backed one wheel of the trailer off the bridge. It stuck there. It took us fifteen minutes to disconnect the trailer from the car and to unstick it from the bridge. It took at least fifteen more minutes to get the calf into the trailer. It weighed at least five-hundred pounds. James had not trained it to climb into a trailer and it had never seen a car up close. It was unwilling to get close to either, let alone getting into the trailer.

By the time we got the calf in the trailer, James' white shirt was so dirty that Mama said he could not show his champion calf looking like that. What would the people think of a mother who sent her son to the Beckham County Fair to show his prize calf looking like that. She rushed into the house and brought out his other shirt right out of the ironing basket. It has been sprinkled down the night before for ironing. When she shook it out, it too was so wrinkled that no self-respecting mother would allow her son to show a calf in it at any kind of a fair.

Calamities on that day seemed to never end. Mom, believing that the calf would get to the fair too late for the judging, had just begun to cry a little when Mr. Martin heard a hissing sound. One of the cold patches on the innertube of the right trailer wheel came loose and we had a flat and no spare tire.

Then Mama just sorta collapsed on the running board of that Model-A, put her face in her hands and cried out loud. Then Mary and Ruth began bellowing. They were almost making music; sad music I might add. All that effort, all that feed, all that training had gone down the drain. There would be no Champion, no Reserve Grand Champion, no Grand Champion, not even a white ribbon.

We got the calf out of the trailer more easily than we got it in. As James led it back to the cow lot, I walked beside him. I looked up and saw tears streaming down his face. The hopes of entering and winning just a ribbon, maybe a blue ribbon, were dashed. Mama's canned peaches did win a red ribbon, but that was little consolation.

On Saturday, Uncle Earl agreed to take both Rowland families down to the fair on his old flatbed Model-T truck. We looked forward to seeing all the exhibits, but mostly we anticipated the carnival. At breakfast that morning, Dad said that each of us could spend no more than fifty cents at the fair. That would be five rides or a combination of rides and shows, hamburgers, Cokes and cotton candy. You could expect freak tents where the fattest woman in the world was displayed or the two-headed cow, or the world's hairiest man. There would be the hall of mirrors, the terror chamber and the ball and coin tosses. The show that most boys wanted to see, but were prohibited from seeing, was the Hootchi Cootchi show — exotic dancing.

Traveling this year with the carnival was a tent with a boxing ring and the show's boxer who was willing to take on all comers.

By ten o'clock everybody from the Riverview Community who was coming to the fair had arrived. Harrel Ray, Goober, Huck and I had already hooked up. By lunch I had spent thirty cents and was wondering what to do with the rest of my money.

We went by the boxing tent and noticed the professional boxer who had agreed to take on all comers, up to five locals. He looked like he weighed about one-hundred and seventy pounds, a light heavyweight. That was about what my dad weighed.

Now my dad was known around the county as a pretty good boxer. He wasn't afraid of anybody and his friends knew it. At one o'clock an announcer came out front with a microphone and challenged anybody, no matter their weight, to take on the carnival professional. Anyone beating him would be awarded a ten dollar bill. Bob Hunter and Uncle Earl encouraged Dad to challenge him. The barker continued to harangue the locals as sissys and cowards. "Who couldn't use a crisp ten dollar bill?" he taunted, waving one above his head.

There were a couple of guys who had had a few shots of rot-gut whiskey that accepted the barker's challenge. Their whiskey had given them a lot of courage. They would start the fights at two o'clock. "Any more takers?" the barker asked. "If any man here can stay in the ring with Slugger McCormack for three rounds, we'll give him five dollars. If anyone beats Slugger, we'll give you ten dollars. You don't get that kind of an offer every day."

Dad had been thinking it over and now a half-dozen guys were-saying, "You can whip him, Sherman." "That guy doesn't look very tough." "He'll be worn out by the time he takes on those two guys, then you can whip him easily."

Dad had a reputation of not being afraid of anyone to protect. The appeal to his pride was so compelling that it was just too much for him. He had thought it over and decided he couldn't lose. If he beat the professional, he would be considered the best boxer in Beckham County and ten dollars richer. If he lost, he lost to a professional. Who could fault him for that? He raised his hand and said, "I'll take him on."

The news spread quickly. The men from around Erick began gathering at the ticket booth and paying twenty-five cents each to get a seat. Boys got in for a dime.

When Mama heard the news, she was chagrined. "How dare you get in the ring with a professional and maybe get your brains knocked out! Don't you realize that you have six kids to feed?" But it didn't change his mind. The sin of the pride of life ruled his brain. He had raised his hand and there would be no chickening out. He would fight Slugger even if he left a widow and six orphans.

Marion Dobson, the Christian Advent preacher and Dad's best friend, heard the news and also tried to persuade Dad not to fight. "You are a Christian, Sherman. Jesus said for us to turn the other cheek. Christians should be opposed to violence, not creating it. I'd be ashamed to get into that ring and bring dishonor on the name of Jesus," said Marion. But he could not persuade Dad to change his devilish course.

The first two fights ended in the first and second rounds. Slugger had hardly worked up a sweat. These guys had hit the ring floor in two and four minutes. They would collect no money.

The barker was also the ring announcer and referee. James and I, along with Roy Whitely, Goober and cousins LeeRoy, Roger, Herman and Darrel, were sitting at ringside. Every square foot in the portable bleachers had someone sitting on it and men were standing in the sawdust at the ends. Uncle Earl was in Dad's corner acting as his second. Just before the match began, Marion Dobson worked his way through those who were standing. We all scooched over to let him sit between LeeRoy and me. He told us he bought a ticket just so he could be there to help in case Sherman got hurt. He was motivated only by pure Christian compassion and brotherly love.

The barker announced that the fight was for three rounds of three minutes each. There would also be a one minute rest period between rounds. In the blue corner, Sherman Rowland of Erick was introduced and Jim "Slugger" McCormack of St. Louis, Missouri, was in the red corner. Everybody clapped and shouted when Dad was introduced and they booed Slugger.

The barker added that if the fight lasted the three rounds, Sherman Rowland was guaranteed a prize of five dollars. And if Sherman Rowland wins, he'll get a prize of ten dollars. James asked Marion what would happen if no one knocked the other out and Dad lasted the full three rounds. Marion replied, "Slugger will win because the barker was also the judge and referee. No one else has a vote."

That wasn't fair, but at least Dad had a chance by knocking him out and winning ten dollars, or going the distance and getting five dollars.

The bell rang and the fight was on. The two fighters circled each other, throwing a few punches that for the most part landed on the gloves of the other. I was impresed with my dad's ability. He was ducking, weaving and shooting his left at Slugger's chin. Occasionally one would land on Slugger's face. Our gang was shouting and screaming and throwing punches in the air as if it would help Dad land his. In three minutes the round ended. As Dad came to his corner, he looked down, smiled, winked at us, and sat down on a stool. Boy, oh boy, we were proud. He was still on his feet at the bell and wasn't bleeding. Uncle Earl hovered over him in the corner and we could hear Uncle Earl shouting, "Throw some rights, Sherman! Throw some rights!" But for some reason, Dad wasn't throwing any rights. Had he sprained his shoulder or busted a knuckle?

Silently I was praying, "Dear God, help Daddy knock him out. We need the ten dollars." I think James was praying, too. I got my inspiration to pray out of need and out of observing Marion Dobson. At the end of the round he bowed his head, closed his eyes and began praying out loud. He was giving thanks that Dad wasn't dead and he was asking God to keep him safe. It was just like I had heard him pray at least fifty times in Sunday school. He would pray for travelers from our community who were away visiting relatives, even if they weren't ten miles from home. "And Lord, keep all our neighbors who are traveling safe and bring them back unharmed to us again."

The bell rang for the second round. The two boxers met in the center of the ring and continued jabbing and ducking. Slugger was throwing both lefts and rights. Marion got into the fight in this round and got away from his praying. When the fighters were mixing it up, he was shouting, "Kill him Sherman, kill him!" But when the round was over, it was still about even.

Everyone in our row seemed to have thrown a lot more punches in the air than the two boxers in the ring had thrown. The Christian Advent preacher was also getting into the fight. He was shouting at the top of his lungs when the round ended and throwing imaginary punches at Slugger. He had never preached with that kind of emotion or that loud in his life.

Dad returned to his corner and gave us another wink and smile. That gave me hope and confidence. He wasn't getting hurt, at least not in the first two rounds. Marion said, "This is the round when your dad is going to get a boxing lesson and we will see some blood." That scared me. I wanted to shout, "Daddy, forget the ten dollars, even the five. It's not going to be worth it." But I didn't. My hope was that Daddy could get through the fight unscathed and win the five dollars.

All of us could hear Uncle Earl pleading with Dad, "Throw some rights, Sherman! Please throw some rights!" What he, and we, didn't know was that Dad was saving his right. He wanted to let Slugger McCormack think he had nothing but a left hand and could throw only left jabs and hooks.

The minute rest ended and the bell rang. We were all hoping that Dad could just finish the final round so we could go home with the five dollars. Who cared if Dad really won? The main thing was, don't get hurt. I was pleading for Dad to duck and weave and run for three more minutes, even if he didn't land one punch.

The bell sounded and Slugger crossed the ring with killing in his eyes. What he didn't know was that Dad had a secret punch. He shot his left hand out and down, making sort of a corkscrew out of his left arm. In fact, it looked kind of deformed. As Slugger reached Dad, Dad uncorked his left arm and sent a blow to Slugger's gut. It didn't seem to hurt him but it did surprise him. They sparred a few more seconds and Slugger landed a couple of solid blows. Then Dad sent his left arm down and out to the side in his corkscrew form and uncorked it with an uppercut right on Slugger's chin. That blow didn't seem to hurt him any either, but it seemed to come from nowhere to Slugger's surprise.

They sparred a little more and again out went the corkscrew. Slugger reached out to block it with both hands leaving his whole head exposed. Dad then crossed with a vicious right to Slugger's chin followed by a corkscrew hook and another right cross. Slugger's knees buckled and he hit the canvas on his face. The referee was astonished! Dad went to a neutral corner and a slow count was started. But the referee reached ten. (He could have counted on to a slow twenty and it would have made no difference.)

The local crowd was delirious! Men and boys were jumping and screaming at the tops of their lungs. They were ready to tear the place down. The commotion was so great that everybody else who was not in the middle of a game, ride or at the freak show, rushed to the boxing ring tent to see what was happening. Women by the score rushed to the front of the boxing tent. Uncle Earl stood in Dad's corner tottaly stunned. But, the most interesting thing that happened immediately after the ten-count, was that Marion Dobson rushed through the ropes and into the ring. He grabbed Dad's right hand and lifted it above Dad's head and paraded him around the ring for five minutes. You would have thought the boxing match was his idea. Beckham County had a new hero and he was my dad.

The dust settled down from the boxing match and congratulations were abundantly poured on Dad's head. Then Goober, Harrel Ray Huck and I got together and went around to the front of the Hootchi Cootchi tent. It was staked away from the main carnival esplonage. It was around the corner and behind the boxing tent. The canvas sign across the front invited the crowd to come to the most exciting exotic show in Oklahoma. It had a picture of a scantily clothed woman with lots of skin showing. The slogan across the top of the sign read, "SEE MISS TITLYWINKS-EXOTIC DANCER." We knew our moms would not be there and doubted that our dads would even come around that corner where the boxing tent stood.

Most of the church people didn't want that show in the county fair but it was part of the contract signed by the Beckham County Fair Association and the carnival owners. So the show was permitted to go on.

The four of us went around the corner, not to see who was buying tickets and going to the show, but in hopes of getting a glimpse of Miss

Titlywinks. A barker was encouraging the men gathered in front to see the show and "get yourself rejuvenated." It seemed that the men buying tickets were single guys in their twenties and husbands who had come to the fair alone.

The four of us stood there peeking through the curtain flaps over the doorway every time someone pushed them back to enter the tent, hoping to get a peek at the star. We did finally get to see Miss Titlywinks as the barker was trying to convince a few more men to buy tickets. She briefly opened the flaps and looked out. She was wearing what looked like a bathing suit under some pink and blue strips of gauze. She was pretty well painted and it was obvious, even to us boys, that she was a sinner. She gave the crowd a sexy smile and a big wink. She crooked her index finger and jestered for the men to come on in. Her appearance in the door of the tent convinced a dozen more men to buy tickets and they rushed through the door.

We boys lingered around until the music started blaring through the tent walls. Huck suggested that we go around to the back of the tent and listen. We liked his suggestion and did just that. The men would stomp their feet and shout as she apparently removed each layer of gauze or clothing. We couldn't see, but we could imagine. Huck suggested that if two of us grabbed the bottom of the tent and lifted it up, the other two could sneak a peek and no one would ever know. If we did it when the men were shouting and stomping and everyone's eyes were on Miss Titlywinks, they wouldn't even see us peeking.

I thought it was a pretty good idea, but I told the others I could not look and lust after that woman. But, I would hold up the bottom of the tent so the other ones could. That way they could tell me what they saw and I wouldn't be guilty of the lust of the flesh or the lust of the eyes. I had never heard any preacher say that there was a lust of the ears, so listening to what they saw would be OK. I was making a great sacrifice in the name of righteousness. It was agreed that Goober and I would yank the bottom of the tent up while Huck and Harrel Ray got to lust after the forbidden fruit.

They got down on their bellies in the dirt and Goober and I bent over and pulled the tent bottom up. Harrel Ray and Huck found themselves looking through a dozen legs and could hardly see the stage. After a minute, Goober and I said that's enough. But both of them kept trying to get their heads farther into the tent. They wouldn't back out, so Goober dropped on his knees and forced his head under for a peek. The excitement of the moment, the conflict between maybe seeing Miss Titlywinks stripped down to the bare flesh and my conscience forced me to make a quick decision. I wish it had been a righteous one, but it wasn't. I knew how the Disciples felt in the garden, "My spirit was willing, but my flesh was weak."

I dropped down on my knees, too. I forced my head under the tent and all I could see was the backs of men's shoes, boots and pants legs. Just as I was getting my eyes adjusted enough to pick out a little of Miss Titlywinks, someone yelled, "What are you boys doing?" We turned to see the biggest, dirtiest, ugliest and meanest looking man you could ever imagine. His face was pock marked, he had snaggled teeth and he was carrying a bull whip. He was a Carnie and his job was to see that no one snuck into the shows. He popped that whip in the air and we took off like bats out of hell in every direction running into and stumbling over the tent ropes. He scared us half to death. If he had lashed me with that whip, I wouldn't have complained because I had compromised my convictions. Worse yet, I didn't even get one peek at Miss Titlywinks. The other guys could brag about what them claimed to have seen, or thought they had seen, but I had nothing to report but how scared I was.

The day was ending and the fair would soon be over. We piled onto Uncle Earl's flat-bed truck and headed home. Dad was ten dollars richer and was now a hometown hero. Mom never criticized him again for thinking he could beat the professional, even though she had put up a big protest before the fight.

When we got home there were cows to be milked, horses to be fed, hogs to be slopped, wood to be cut and water to be carried to the house before we went to bed. But we could look forward to next year's County Fair and all the fun that goes with it.

What we would need to make the fair perfect, would be enough money to take in every ride and see every show, except of course, Miss Titlywink's.

CHAPTER 14
WINTER'S CHALLENGES

Winter brought challenges like no other season. Every season brought good things and sometimes they brought bad things. There was the bank loan made every spring that was spent to put in that year's crops. It had to be paid at the end of cotton harvest. There were fresh vegetables from the garden to eat in the late spring and summer. There were canned ones for the fall and the winter. There was some WPA money in the summer, but they didn't always build roads in the winter. There was some money from barbering, picking and selling cotton in the fall. Most winters, we had faced Christmas with a little hope. The winter of 1936, my sixth grade year, was the bleakest. Nearly every Christmas in my memory was filled with some joy and expectation. We had always hung our stockings on the wall behind our heating stove on Christmas Eve. Somehow, Dad and Mom had found the money to buy some hard candy and a few assorted nuts, like pecans, walnuts, and Brazil nuts, to put in our stockings. They had also put an orange and an apple in each sock. Each child also received some kind of a toy, even if it only cost a dime. We never had a real Christmas tree. This year Mom was determined to relieve the bleakness of our poverty.

She sent James and me out to cut off a big branch off the mulberry tree to decorate. We did, and it had not one leaf on it. It did have a bunch of barren crooked limbs, though. We had some popcorn and Mom popped it in the skillet. It was not for eating but was used to decorate the tree. Mary and Ruth took needles and thread and made long strings of popcorn. These were threaded in, around and over the barren limbs of the branch we had set up in the living room. Mom then cut thin strips of green and red crepe paper, and hung them over the limbs. She had saved the lids of tin cans and fruit jars, so she had us punch holes in them and hang them on the bush. These lids reflected light and moved a bit when the air was stirred as someone walked by or the door was closed. When we finished the decorating, it wasn't a fir, but we still had a Christmas tree. To us it was as pretty as any evergreen tree that some folks in town were able to afford.

That had been a bad year for our animals, garden, feed crops and cotton. The drought killed most of our crops, or caused them to produce little or nothing of value. A grasshopper plague hit in late summer and ate up what was left of our garden and most of the feed crops that were still alive. We mixed bran, syrup and arsenic and spread it out in the fields just like Taylor and Jimmy demonstrated. But, faster than it killed the grasshoppers on our place they were replaced. Every gust of stiff wind would bring swarms of new ones from neighboring farms. They were so thick that they looked like a cloud approaching. They just couldn't be stopped or killed off. We had no choice but to yield to their devastation.

Money was so scarce that Dad had to take half of the twenty-five cents a hundred we were paid for picking cotton on other farms to meet family expenses. He could only pay us half the going rate when we picked what was left of our own cotton. There was barely enough money left from our earnings to buy our winter clothes. We picked cotton all day, every day, and made less than twenty cents a day after sharing with Daddy. James made a little more but it wasn't much more.

Christmas fell on Sunday that year. The weather was cold and windy. On the Saturday before Christmas, Dad, James and I were the only ones who went to town. Dad took care of the usual business, selling the cream and two dozen eggs. He went to the grocery store and bought the necessities for our table — sugar, flour, beans, corn meal and oats for breakfast.

That day, business was brisk at Mr. Ray's grocery, so he hired Dad to sack groceries for a couple of hours. I say hired, but it was not for money. He told Daddy that he could go by his house and pick up some toys for the children in exchange for his help. James and I watched Dad pretty closely that day. We hoped to see him go to the variety store, because that would mean that he was going to buy some toys for us. None of the four oldest children believed in Santa Claus, nor had we since we were about five years old. But, we all believed that somehow, some way, Dad and Mom had saved some money for Christmas. This year they had none.

When Mr. Ray closed the store, he told Dad to go by his house and speak to his wife. We drove the wagon up the Ray's house, got down, walked up to the house and knocked on the door. Mrs. Ray came to the door and invited us in. There on the living room floor were a number of useful used items, along with some used toys. She told James and me to pick out one toy or gift for each of our brothers and sisters and one for ourselves.

We eyed the toys and picked out a little tin tractor for Rick. We chose a Raggedy Ann Doll for Jo. Ruth and Mary were going to get used hair brushes. James picked out a used beaded belt for himself. I chose an old inflatable donkey made of rubber, like the kind you would find in an inner tube. You could inflate it by blowing into its tail. When inflated you would bend the tail over and tie it with string to help keep the air in. When fully inflated it would stand on its own four feet. I could never tie the tail tight enough to keep the air from leaking out. As the air leaked out, the mules legs began to bend and it would finally flop over on the floor. I don't know how many times I blew that donkey up. But, I would be able to remember the stench of the air it exhausted for the rest of my life.

Dad had bought a pound of hard candy. Neither Mom nor Dad received a single gift from each other. They did have each other's love and devotion. Christmas was always a challenge. That year those used gifts and few pieces of hard candy were most appreciated. It was to be our last Christmas in Oklahoma. It had been a challenge, but we made it through the holidays. The Rays had made it better than it would have otherwise been. Their charitable spirit left a lasting impression on me. We were not the only family in the community that had a bit of Christmas that year instead of none. Other poor parents knocked on their door that Christmas Eve and were given something to break the dreariness of that Christmas.

Another of winter's challenges was the annual spread of the itch. During the winter months, as in the summer, we wore our clothes all week long. In the summer months we just wore our shirts and our pants. By thanksgiving we boys were wearing long handles.

The girls were wearing flannel bloomers that came down to their knees and long cotton stockings that were held up by rubber garters. These under garments were not washed as often as our regular clothes because we had only one set of them. Nearly every winter one or all of us got the itch. The skin under our arms and in our crotches would start chaffing. Then it would spread to other areas of our bodies. It itched and we scratched. As we scratched, our skin turned red and tender. We sometimes scratched so hard that it brought blood. That winter we all caught the itch. Some of us had it worse than the others.

There was one country remedy that everybody relied on to kill the itch. It was a mixture of lard and sulfur. When the first kid showed up at school with the itch, everyone else in school knew it. We could smell the sulfur, especially when we came in to the schoolroom to warm ourselves around the large pot-bellied stove.

This winter, Ruth was the first one in our family to get the itch. It quickly spread over half of her body. She was barely able to keep from scratching it when she was awake, but she couldn't control the scratching when she was asleep. Some of the spots turned red and bloody. Scabs formed on them. Mom sewed her a pair of flannel mittens to wear at night to keep her from hurting herself worse when she was asleep. The sulfur and lard weren't doing the job on her though. Dad sought other remedies.

When discussing it with a neighbor, he recommended a Poke root solution. He said that we should dig up some roots from Poke plants and boil them. Then he said to bathe Ruth to remove the sulfur and lard, then wash her with the water from the boiled roots. We had a number of Poke plants growing in some of our Shinnery patches. Dad sent James and me with the shovel to the patches to dig up the roots of the Poke plants. These Poke plants provided a delicacy, known as Poke Salad, during their growing season.

There were about two inches of snow on the ground and it was as cold as blue blazes. James and I brought back the pile of roots, and Mom boiled them in the pressure cooker on the stove. Mother put Ruth in a wash tub, bathed her real well and then started pouring the Poke root water over her body. When the water ran over her chapped and itchy skin, it set her on fire. She started screaming so loud that it scared everyone in the house half to death.

Daddy rushed into the kitchen to see what had happened. Ruth was standing naked in the wash tub in terrible pain. When she wouldn't quit screaming, he picked her up, rushed her to the front yard and rolled her in the snow. The snow shocked Ruth into silence and it cooled the burning from the Poke root cure.

Daddy was so mad at the neighbor for recommending the Poke remedy that he wanted to go down to his place and punch him out. He said if he had wanted to put her in pain, he would have taken her to a sheep dip, because Creosote couldn't have been any worse.

The itch would go from one kid to the next during the winter months. The best protection was the regular washing of our clothes, especially our underclothes. But the itch wasn't the only thing we were afflicted with in the winter. Lice could be just as bad or worse.

The big problem with lice was that they could spread and multiply so easily. They laid their eggs, called nits, by the hundreds. When one kid in school got them, it seemed that every kid had them in a couple of weeks.

The source of their contamination was varied. I got them one time carrying an opossum by the tail. I caught it in one of my traps and about half way back to the house I noted something sort of itching or biting on my wrist and forearm. I looked down and it seemed like a million lice were deserting that dead opossum via its tail and crawling up my arm. I couldn't keep carrying it and allow those lice to take up a habitat on my body. I dropped the varmint and raced home and wiped my body down with coal oil. Then I got a piece of bailing wire that I took back and tied around the opossum's neck to drag it home. I didn't want to get anymore lice. I waited until the next day to skin it when all the lice were gone.

During school days we wrestled, snatched and wore each other's caps. There weren't five pocket combs in the whole school, but the vain ones borrowed combs from each other to keep their hair in place. Each of these activities passed on the lice, or their nits, until the whole school was infested with them. Someone was always blamed for introducing them, usually the poorest and most defenseless family in the community.

Any one could start the infestation. Our old hens often carried lice. Their nests had lice. Dogs and cats could be carriers. When it came to the infested human beings, the only remedies were soapy baths and getting wiped down with coal oil. Dad would cut us boys' hair real short and then rub coal oil on our scalps. It took about three treatments to kill all the lice.

The sulfur and coal oil are other odors that I would also remember all my life. All those winters were hard and we had endured about all of them we could take. This winter was the worst. Something was going to have to give. We could not endure another year like this one.

CHAPTER 15
SELLING OUT AND HEADING WEST

One night, early in March, Dad told us that we were going to lose the team of mules unless we came up with the money to at least pay the interest on the loan he had taken out on them. The interest alone was going to run twenty-one dollars. He had sold all the cotton we had picked and it didn't even pay off the whole loan on last year's crop. He had pledged the mules on a second loan. I had just sold my pelts and had nearly ten dollars of trapping money left. James had about the same amount. The high school principal had paid him for taking care of his cattle after school in January and February. The principal was enrolled in some night courses at Southwestern State College in Weatherford and had to go there three nights a week. He hired James to do the evening chores on those nights.

We went into the room we slept in and got all our money and gave it to Dad. Tears welled up in his eyes, as he thanked and hugged us. But the bank wasn't satisfied with just the interest payment and would soon be back for more.

Dad and Mom couldn't make the full bank loan payments on any of the loans. They had pledged their interest in Grandpa Rowland's farm as collateral when they bought our place. Foreclosure would mean that we would lose our interest in both properties. It seemed obvious to everyone that the drought could continue to get worse. No amount of praying or tongue speaking was going to change it. The dust storms seemed to get bigger and more frequent.

After supper a few days later, Dad and Mama announced that we were going to sell out and turn the farms over to the bank. We would have an auction sale and pay off the mule loan. They said the bank wasn't going to grant any more extensions. After the sale, we would have to start to California. We had no other choice.

Half the families in the community had sold out or were in the process of doing so. Every edition of the *Beckham County Democrat* advertised three or four farm auction sales. Everybody hoped to get enough money to buy a car or truck and have enough money left over to get to California. Fine workhorses and mules that would have brought a hundred fifty dollars four years before were going for twenty-five to thirty-five dollars. You nearly had to give away plows. Scrap metal of all kinds was being sold to junk dealers to be shipped to Japan.

We had our sale and almost everything sold. Nearly all our farm equipment was sold as scrap to the junk dealer by the pound and it was hauled off in a big truck. As our horses and mules were auctioned off, tears were brought to our eyes. I cried when old Tony was led down the lane to the road to be gone forever. I had ridden him countless miles. He was often my companion as I raced down to and across the river bottom to bring up the cows. I had enjoyed a thousand imaginary trips across the silver screen chasing and shooting outlaws from his back with imagined six-shooters. I would never see or ride him again.

Our big mule, Kate, brought the highest price of any of our animals — thirty-five dollars. Next to Tony, I had ridden her more than any other horse or mule. She could run fast, and when coming to a water hole or a creek, she was the only riding animal we had that could and would jump across it. These jumps always brought me great delight. I was going to miss her, too.

As the buyers led the last of our livestock down our lane and away on the country road, I saw Mom standing at the front window crying. The rose bushes she had planted by the window were putting on leaves and buds. She had watered and cared for them for years. But, she would never smell them, or see them bloom again.

The dream of making it as farmers in the sandy hills of Riverview Community was dashed forever. All the efforts and sacrifices had come to naught. The only things left in our house were a table, two cane bottom chairs, three mattresses and the cook stove. We had our clothes, what there was of them, stacked in the corners and along the walls. We also had our silverware, cooking utensils and dishes.

There was one animal that did not sell. It was old Sway. This old Jersey cow was so named because of her terribly swayed back. But she had delivered a calf every year for a decade or more. I had milked her hundreds of times, and she had given us thousands of gallons of milk that we drank, after skimming the cream off the top to sell at the creamery. The cream from her rich milk, along with that of three other cows, had always brought in a small amount of cash. It had determined many times whether or not we would have sugar, baking powder, flour, corn meal, Mother's Oats and medicines or not.

Old Sway was on her last leg. When she got down she could hardly get up, even to eat or drink. She died in the barn the night before we left for California. We had no team to drag her out to the pasture, so she was left to rot right there in the barn. The bank had the farm, let them drag her out if they wanted to.

Her dead bloated carcass seemed to represent the end of our past hopes and dreams. They had been dying for years, but on that day they died with old Sway and we were forced to abandon them.

Daddy took the proceeds from the sale and bought an old Model-A flatbed Ford truck. He put a couple of new tires on it and kept the old ones for spares. He built a box about two feet high across the front end of the truck bed to hold our cooking and eating utensils, and our clothes. The three mattresses, when stacked on top of the other, covered the remainder of the truck bed.

Our sheets, blankets, and quilts were stored between the mattresses. There were sideboards on the truck about two feet high, and a ridge pole about five feet high that ran down the middle. A canvas was stretched across the ridge pole and was attached to the sideboards making it look like a tent.

One of our neighbors, Mr. Sparks, who had said he was going to stick it out, came by on our last evening at the house. He took old Peg and Shep. We had decided to take Snowball, the little dog, with us. Daddy was too attached to her to leave her. There were some more tears shed as we kids hugged the two dogs goodbye. Mr. Sparks then led dogs off. They strained at their leashes as he pulled them down the lane to the road and on toward his house. It was goodbye to the dogs we had taken hunting so many times and whose ability to catch rabbits had furnished meat for our table so many of those times. They had faithfully warned us a thousand times when anyone was approaching our house at night or in the daytime.

It was over. The next day Dad and Mom, along with six children and Snowball, headed south on a sandy road. We passed the Buchannons, the empty Morris house, the empty Jones house, the schoolhouse, the empty Whitely house, and the empty Williams house. The Dobson house was the last one before turning onto US 66. We stopped to say goodbye to them. Marion had been Dad's closest friend since childhood, even if they didn't always agree on religion and politics. They knew that they might never see each other again. Everybody was hugging and even kissing each other goodbye. Dad and Marion were shedding tears unabashedly, so it was all right for all of us to cry. So we all did.

We loaded up, waved goodbye and started out. The ruts on the road were so deep that Dad didn't even have to steer the truck. We turned west off that sandy road on to US Highway 66. It was a concrete road that would take us to California if our money didn't run out before we got there. Our top speed would be forty miles an hour where the highway was level.

When we reached Texola, situated on the Texas line, there was a big sign across the side of the town's only gas station. It read, "Fill up now! Gas is Higher in Texas." We did. We would be known as and called from then on, "Okies." We were not described very well by John Steinbeck in his book, *The Grapes of Wrath*, for which he won the Pulitzer Prize in 1940. But, we wore the name "Okie" with pride.

Later, when it was used disparagingly by the prune pickers in California to put us down, we would put up our fists and defend our Oklahoma heritage against anybody. I'd have a dozen or more fist-fights over that name. So would James. No one would insult us, or bully us around again. Never! Yes, we were poor "Okies" heading west, but Mama and Daddy would make sure that we never lost our faith in God and ourselves, or our dignity.